A mo

on the door and

recorder, and several cellophane wrappers lay sea...

on the long table. He flicked his gaze away from the inanimate objects and discovered one person, a woman in gray pants and navy jacket, standing at the coffee maker. His lips froze before a greeting escaped.

Her? She works for the police? A detective? Fragile dreams of shared runs, quiet meals, and warm embraces spun during the past two nights vanished. Apprehension, his internal beast, stood at attention in the curve of his stomach, a carved stone gaining weight by the second.

"Have a seat, Dr. Holmes. My partner stepped out for a few minutes, but we can get started. Coffee? Water?" Maylee turned and inspected him over the rim of a paper cup.

Detective. Female. Gun. He swallowed back the primal cry climbing his throat. The trifecta of terror stood five feet away. Once upon a time...until Dr. DeVino told him his boss was dead and detectives needed statements, it had been a better than average day. He shook his head before claiming the nearest metal and fiberglass chair. "This"—he gestured to include the entire room—"is an awkward way to learn your occupation."

Praise for Ellen Parker

"Beautifully written and enjoyable to read."

~Jeanne Thomas

~*~

"I liked that my daughter could read it when I finished."

~Barb Dempsey

~*~

"Parker tells a tale that is light and entertaining with a good dose of 'what will happen next.'"

~Pure Jonel

Stare Down

by

Ellen Parker

Stare Down

Cover Art by *Debbie Taylor*

The Wild Rose Press, Inc.
PO Box 708
Adams Basin, NY 14410-0708
Visit us at www.thewildrosepress.com

Publishing History
First Crimson Rose Edition, 2015
Print ISBN 978-1-5092-0400-7
Digital ISBN 978-1-5092-0401-4

Published in the United States of America

Dedication

To the members of
Missouri Romance Writers of America.
Thanks for your on-going education
and encouragement.

Chapter One

A single ambulance screamed into the spring evening as it headed toward the freeway exit parallel to Leine Street. Dr. Dave Holmes didn't break stride, simply satisfied his curiosity with a quick glance to his right. An instant later, he nodded as the sound and lights continued in the direction of Grand Avenue Hospital, a well-known complex of buildings in St. Louis.

Enjoy the few days before my on-call rotation starts. He jogged into Saxon Park making mental plans for the remaining evenings of the week. A decent run topped the list, one item above exploring this park, a convenient three blocks from his new apartment. He followed a narrow path between a dog run and a playground, circled a backless bench, and started his stretching routine.

He reached for his phone on the second chirp. For a heartbeat, he puzzled over the number. It belonged to neither immediate family nor work. It appeared local, a little familiar, but he couldn't put a name to it before he pressed talk. "This is Holmes."

"Exactly the man I wanted to talk to. Do you have a minute?"

"Always for you, Dr. Art." Dave propped one foot on the painted, wooden bench. Dr. Arturo Saterro wore several hats in Dave's life. He'd been teacher, mentor, and friend. Last summer, when Dave passed the general surgical exams, the term colleague expanded the list. Boss, the newest, became official Monday, a mere three days ago.

"I've something for you. A little token I forgot to bring to the clinic. Can you come over to the house tonight?"

Dave switched to stretching the opposite leg. "I thought you'd be headed to Chicago."

"I'll be leaving in the morning."

"I'm starting a run." He calculated jog, shower, and extra time for getting lost in the circles of a South St. Louis subdivision. "Would eight be too late?"

"Excellent choice. Gives me time to pack the car with all the things Luci wants to give our daughter."

He recalled Luci, Mrs. Saterro, as a tiny woman with friendly dark eyes. She'd been the gracious hostess at several medical student and faculty events. According to the photo on Dr. Art's desk, their daughter inherited Luci's beauty. "Are the rumors true? Will you be doing father-of-the-bride duties before long?"

"Labor Day weekend. Luci signed us up for dance lessons this summer. She claims people will watch us at the reception. Personally, I think they'll be watching the bride. I know I will."

"Not the groom?" Dave listened to a faint chuckle. "Well, I've got to run. See you at the house."

"The light will be on."

Dave disconnected the call and finished his stretching routine. A few moments later he adjusted his aviators and jogged to the wide asphalt path encircling Saxon Pond.

A puff of late April breeze carried lilacs in full bloom to him while he rounded the first curve. He frowned at the bushes with bunches of variegated purple blossoms. Sandra wore lilac cologne—year round—in great quantities. He tried to block out his mother's image and find a more pleasant memory. His mind scrolled all the way back to the house in Marshall, Missouri. As a young boy, he, his brother, and their friends spent hours playing with their trucks and action figures in the shade and shelter of the bushes on the property line. They lived as a family then—father, mother, and two boys. In the blink of an eye all their lives changed. Now, lilac perfume slapped him in the face with contrasts between before and after.

Freeway traffic hummed in its artificial valley to his right as he ran toward the setting sun.

"On your left."

He eased to the edge of the path and glanced as the owner of the female voice pulled even with him, then ahead.

Legs. Perfect legs. His heart rate shifted up a gear from more than his running. He forced his gaze upward and found only a scrap of red shorts beneath an extra-long obnoxious green and silver safety vest. Short brunette hair bounced in tempo with her stride. "Hey."

She ignored him.

Deserved that. He settled back into his previous pace and watched her increase the distance between them. The lady ran like a gazelle. Moments later she turned the next corner. His view became limited to glimpses of her standout vest between the statuary, flowerbeds, and other park visitors plentiful along the Grand Avenue side of the park.

Three full laps later, Dave rounded the corner to the long south-side straight and sighed. He'd not even caught a glimpse of Antelope Girl for a lap and a half. He shook his head. Was he considering flirting? Picking up the first long-legged runner in sight?

Never seem to get beyond friend. He shook away the words of another email asking him to "save the date" to attend a wedding of a former classmate.

"On your left."

This time he surged forward before she pulled even. Cousin Aaron would call it seizing the opportunity and tossing his normal social hesitancy aside. "Run together?"

She turned her head and smiled below narrow wrap-around sunglasses. "Can you keep up?"

"Maybe." He stayed pace for pace through the corner. "Training for the Olympics?"

She flashed him another smile. "Fun. You?"

How could he put his usual answer of fitness, weight control, and mental health in words compatible with running at his top speed? "Peer pressure."

"That will do it. Who are they?" She released her words light and spaced.

"There." He gestured off toward Grand Avenue Hospital, a local landmark less than a mile on the other side of the freeway. Clinics, rehab centers, and other entities associated with the medical teaching and research filled several blocks surrounding the primary building. Grand Avenue Surgical Associates, his work home for the foreseeable future, occupied half a floor in one of the modest buildings lost in the maze from here.

"Good guy in a white coat?"

"Name of the goal." He gulped air while pushing

his legs to maintain the pace.

"It's good to have those. Goals."

They ran silent for an entire lap. Dave became aware of every drop of sweat oozing out of his hairline and taking a crooked path down his neck. His shirt clung to him like a wet, unwelcome second skin. He glanced at her. The only visible sign of exertion on her face remained a faint sheen of perspiration. Her loose vest concealed most of her body, giving him only a hint of a pale knit shirt over feminine curves. Did she live in the neighborhood? Run here often? Always this intense? "How many laps?"

"Depends." She eased back as they curved near the lilacs.

"Today."

"Final one."

"How…" His breath preferred run or talk, not both. "…often?"

"In an ideal world?"

He nodded, willing to let her talk while he stayed even.

"Three…four times a week."

"Live close?"

"This is where I leave." She smiled wide enough to display even teeth and pointed to the next path, the one winding between playground and dog run to Leine Street.

"By the way…" He panted, as he slackened the pace. "I'm Dave."

She smiled once more before starting down the narrower paved strip. She'd taken half a dozen long strides away from him before she tossed a single word over her shoulder. "Maylee."

****

Maylee Morgan curved her lips into a broad smile as she trotted toward home. *By all the hair on a Saint Bernard!* Dave, the long-haired blond, forced a hard run. She worked hard to lap him after passing him on the westbound portion. A man with his speed and endurance could make a good running partner as she prepared for the Poppy Run at the end of May.

If, no, better to think positive—when she saw him again, she'd pose the question. Exercise buddies could be difficult to keep with her unpredictable work hours. A medical man, definitely a step away from cops, the one profession she shied away from in her social life.

A block from the apartment she tapered to a brisk walk as her phone started playing "How Dry I Am." "Afternoon, Kate."

"What's new in the world of law enforcement?" Kate Allegro opened the conversation over a background of male voices and a muffled motor.

"It's the same old thing. Stupid humans break the rules and get arrested." Maylee recited her standard description of police work while imagining her friend taking a break amid piles of mulch, topsoil, and bright white crushed stone. As assistant manager at a landscape and garden center, Kate dealt with a slightly different set of stupid people daily. "Or do you want me to be more specific?"

"Did you do any of the arresting today?"

Maylee sighed, entered the brick apartment building, and started up the stairs to the second floor. "Today, I paced the halls of the courthouse. No matter how well they think they have witnesses scheduled, a person waits hours to answer a few minutes of questions."

"A detective case?"

"Not yet. The real world moves slower than *Law & Order*. My promotion to detective was only four months ago." She had celebrated her promotion and twenty-ninth birthday in the same month, putting a firm stamp on both newest and youngest detective in the department. She let her brain take a quick inventory of the cases she and her training partner had investigated and sent to the city attorney as her hands unlocked the apartment door. The cases waited in various stages for either plea arrangements or trials. Today's testimony concerned an arrest on patrol, a man who forced a foot chase when he bolted from a stolen car. "So…tell me something from your world."

"The couch gardeners have arrived in full force. Three sunny days in a row, and I'm tempted to wager every house in the county will have petunias and geraniums by tomorrow."

"Everyone except my landlord."

"You're in the city."

"Lest I forget?" She sighed. Her city job included a residency requirement. Large portions of her family and friends used the fact as a springboard for all sorts of jokes—most tinged with dark humor.

"Do you have plans for Saturday?"

Maylee shed her vest. A moment later she plucked Angel, her Glock 19, from her hip holster and laid it on a small, round dinette table. "It's too early to tell. What do you have planned?"

"A couple of us are going to the International Festival. We could use your keen eye to help us assess the men."

"My record's skewed to elimination, not encouragement of relationships longer than an hour." Maylee tended to have a natural lie detector when meeting new people. Kate and a few other friends described it as a protective mechanism developed by living with her brothers. But several times it spotted padded resumes and caused her to cut relationships short. Professionally, it gave her a slight advantage during interrogations. On the personal side of her life, she treated it as a survival instinct.

"One of these days, Mr. Wonderful will find you." Kate sounded very sure of her statement.

"With my luck, he'll wear a police uniform," Maylee replied.

"The world would not end."

Maylee didn't feel as confident on this subject as her friend. She'd observed too many relationships between officers crumble from the natural stress of the job and scheduling difficulties. So she practiced negative responses when fellow officers invited her to be their "guest" or "plus one." She pulled out the first frozen entrée her hand encountered and began prepping it for the microwave. "We need to find out where the culinary students hang out. Then I wouldn't be testing smoke alarms when I attempt baking."

"And I'd keep the rest of my fingers."

"That is one advantage." She thought of Kate two years ago fixing supper for a date and ending the evening in the emergency room. Her boyfriend of the month took both Kate and the tip of her index finger to the hospital where the surgeons made a valiant effort to reattach the digit. In the end, both the surgical and emotional attachments failed.

"About Saturday," Kate muttered a few words away from the phone.

"It's too soon to tell. I won't really know until about noon. Is midday too late?"

"I'll consider you a definite maybe. I have to go. Call me tomorrow. I heard from my new electronic pen pal again."

"It's a promise." *Electronic pen pal.* No, she added her phone to the gun and badge on the table and crossed off the Internet dating and mating services as viable. The level of deception on most of the sites made the suspects and witnesses she questioned appear as shiny examples of virtue. She'd go with face-to-face contact.

Maylee sauntered over to the dining area window and glanced down at the parking lot. Assigned parking spots put her silver Camry next to the Prius belonging to the new resident. *Looks like a tangerine.*

The small orange car first appeared Sunday night.

Monday, when she'd returned from work, Mrs. Gossen waylaid her in the hall. The elderly woman lived downstairs in 104 and kept tabs on all the comings and goings in this building plus the one across the street. Maylee regarded her neighbor as more interesting and detailed than the neighborhood newspaper. The elderly widow shared pages of opinion flavored with information. Her monologue two days ago included the fact apartment 102 had a new resident. Three "nice young men" moved things in Sunday.

"They started and finished before I could get a proper welcome organized; hardly a sound from the other side of the wall since. Wonder where he works? Handsome young man." Maylee repeated several key phrases to the empty apartment. Considering the description came from Mrs. Gossen, "young" could refer to anyone still having all their own hair and teeth.

She started to turn away, gave another glance outside, and froze.

A man in dark shorts and faded red shirt crossed the parking lot, stopped at the Prius, and removed a multi-use shopping bag from the rear storage compartment. He glanced up at the building for an instant before walking to the back door.

Maylee sucked in air and held it. Was it? What next? She stared out at the spot until the microwave called her back to the task at hand. She headed for the kitchen, letting her mind whirl with worn and corny ideas of how to properly introduce herself to Dave, the blond runner.

Chapter Two

Maylee held her breath as she lifted the thin green plastic a second time. She moved one gloved hand in a wider arc, exposing more of the victim's head. Why did so many people die with open eyes? She forced her gaze to move to other features of the adult, white male's face. Shallow cuts marred the victim's forehead, cheek and chin. "Not much blood."

"Tell me more." Detective Tom Wilson squatted on the opposite side of the body.

She responded as a rookie, or student, should to his greater experience. Her mind pushed the sounds of more vehicles arriving into the background where they belonged. She pressed her lips tight, delayed a moment by studying the short cemetery grass around the victim, and finally resting her gaze on the light rope binding a shower curtain into a shroud. Two of three knots remained intact, one near the midpoint and the other tight enough around ankles to hint at the feet below. An hour ago, flapping plastic where it didn't belong caught the groundskeeper's attention and he called 911 after a quick look.

"I don't think this is our crime scene. We need to find the actual site of the murder. Where the blood pool will be." Fine lines. Narrow blade. Box cutter?

"Or?" Tom prodded.

"The cuts may be post mortem." She glanced again

at the wounds filled with faint, rust colored, dried blood. Fresh injuries on the face, including shallow ones, would bleed profusely, but they wouldn't kill.

She levered up and stared off down the rows of grave markers. Early afternoon sun encouraged her to squint as her thoughts discarded the facial wounds as more than a symbol or statement. *Why here?* All Saints Cemetery sprawled over eighty acres at the southern edge of St. Louis. The graves went back well over a hundred years. Dozens of the oldest were moved out here as the city expanded in the nineteenth century. The new, active portion of the grounds lay off to the west, where the stones stood almost uniform and in straighter rows. "Either way, I think the body's been moved."

"Exactly my thoughts. Medical examiner should be able to give us more information." Tom stood and brushed bits of grass from his black trousers.

"And time of death." She pushed a leaf aside with her foot to get a better view of the dates on the nearest flat stone. *Victor E. Galati 1889—1953.* Why this place? Did the killer have a message to send by selecting this plot? Or did he panic and pick the first place with a little shelter from the busy street?

She brushed the back of her wrist across her forehead. *A habit to break.* Her new, shorter hairstyle kept the strands out of the way. At the edge of the drive, the cemetery caretaker stood in front of a uniformed officer and gestured as if talking more with hands than mouth. The employee's statement would be important. And they'd need to check where the man spent last night. She pulled out her notebook and began jotting down the names of businesses visible from this position.

"Talk to me, partner." Tom unwrapped a mint with his ungloved hand.

"Prioritizing neighborhood interviews." She moved her gaze to the respected detective three years shy of retirement. Throughout the hours of one shift he morphed from teacher, role model, protector, and faux father. She could do without the last. Lessons from her actual parent didn't vanish with her dad's final breath three years ago. "I'm thinking the pharmacy first and then the restaurant."

"Don't forget the three little storefronts between."

"Nor the apartments across the corner. How many uniforms will assist?" She counted the patrol cars on site and came up short of the personnel numbers to do an accurate, timely canvass. Then, all of a sudden, she shifted her focus to the plain black van turning into the main gate. Eager excitement mixed with sorrow and dread at the knowledge they would soon be removing the shower curtain shroud and learning more about their victim. It would be good if they found identification wrapped with him. She'd gladly delay working on her first John Doe case.

A few minutes later, introductions and the obligatory comment of a dead body in a cemetery complete, they settled in to work. Maylee, Tom, the assistant medical examiner, and an evidence collection specialist surrounded the victim.

"Figures. Organized criminals make our job more difficult." Tom leaned in for another photo of the nude man's hands. "Go ahead and roll prints now, but I don't expect much of them."

Maylee studied the fine cuts on the victim's hands. They appeared to have been made by the same or similar knife used to mutilate the face. Both body sites bore a pattern of intersecting straight lines. The design reminded her of an attempt at drawing a diamond pattern when the paper wasn't on a flat surface.

The doctor lifted one hand away from the abdomen and inspected the thumb. "I'll try to get you a better set during autopsy. Body's in full rigor." He consulted a chart and double-checked the readout on a long slender probe inserted into the victim's liver. "Best estimate for time of death is 2200 to 0200."

Midnight, give or take two hours. Maylee let the time frame settle in her mind and expanded it to dawn for the questions in this neighborhood. "Wedding band's still on. We'll need to know any inscription when you remove it."

"On my check list." Dr. Horworth, the assistant medical examiner, gestured for aid to roll the victim from back to side.

Maylee held a thin hip in position while the forensic pathologist gave a thorough visual exam to the victim's posterior.

"No obvious injuries. Preliminary cause of death will need to wait. But I'm betting you can rule out gunshot or stab wounds. Those"—he pointed to the face—"appear as an afterthought. It might be a tactic to delay identification?"

"How soon will you begin the autopsy?" Maylee stepped aside to make room for the gurney.

"Do you want to watch?" The doctor smiled wide enough to show large, nicotine-stained teeth. "I'm flattered."

She swallowed, hesitated, and tucked her unpleasant memories of morgue visits behind a mental curtain. "Let me rephrase. When should we call to get a preliminary report?"

"I see Detective Wilson is training you well." Dr. Horworth snapped his equipment case closed. "Our gentleman will be first on my list in the morning. Expect an email before noon."

"Thank you." Interviews with the living always won over observing autopsies in her priorities. She exhaled relief as the pathologist and his helper moved toward the van.

A moment later she noticed Tom giving his "walk with me" gesture and followed him across the grass away from the cluster of officials. Had she overstepped?

****

Dave spotted Sandra before the restaurant hostess stepped from behind her podium.

"May I help you?" A young woman dressed in black with the restaurant chain's trademark red and white logo printed on her scarf reached for a menu.

"I'm joining them." He gestured to a lady with rusty curls and a man with a brown plaid shirt side by side in the second booth.

A moment later he slid in opposite the couple.

"David," the woman squealed and extended both arms across the table as if to draw him into a hug.

"In the flesh." He glanced up at the ceiling fan twirling slow and depended on it to dilute Sandra's signature lilac cologne.

"Larry Thompson." The man extended his hand. "Sandra's friend. I figured it was time to meet part of her family."

"Dave. The elder son." He assessed the man's grip

as firm and friendly. A glance at the near stranger's eyes made him decide to delay further opinion.

"I do hope we can do this often. Getting together for supper, I mean." Sandra grasped Dave's wrist for a quick squeeze. "I feel like I never see you."

He pasted on a small smile for her. Every day twice a day wouldn't be often enough if she controlled the world. "I intend on respecting your privacy. I appreciate the same in return."

"Of course." She settled back into the vinyl bench. "I suppose I'll be competing for your attention with your boss, Dr. Saterro."

"Since when did my presence rise to the level of competition? If you're going to keep a running tally, begin with marking off a visit to Dr. Saterro's house last night." Dave managed to give both his drink and food order to the server the moment she finished placing one fish dinner and one grilled chicken special on the table.

"You didn't even look at the menu, David."

"I ate at one of their other locations last week." As usual, his mother changed the topic at the first distraction. He lifted a warm roll from the basket and pulled it apart.

"In Kansas City? With Joseph?"

"Actually, yes. We had a good time during the visit." Dave couldn't remember having a bad time with his brother. Well, a person had to discount a few awkward days during their early teens. After normal rough patches they shared enough of the same interests to enjoy the other's company and careers different enough for the conversation to never get boring.

"I'd like him to move closer." Sandra sprinkled

pepper on her French fries. "Then I'd have both my boys handy."

Dave swallowed back his sigh. Sandra didn't understand—never would understand—she altered the relationship with her sons permanently on one particular August night years ago. Duty and good manners substituted for love and affection from her children. "What about you, Larry? Do you have family in St. Louis?"

"Sister." He pointed to his mouth in a request for patience. "Never married. No children. Do enjoy listening to Sandra brag about her sons."

"I'm proud of my sons. They are two nice, young gentlemen. It's a simple statement of fact." She dabbed tartar sauce on a piece of fish. "Another happens to be we make a good, casual couple."

"Depends how you define casual." Larry finished his water and set the glass where the server would notice. "Thirsty as a catfish today."

Dave studied the other man's hand, no obvious tremble. Good. Sandra tended to collect her male companions at AA meetings. He respected the organization and their aim, but remained aware not all attendees succeeded. The last time he was around when Sandra fell into the gin bottle again, it wasn't pretty.

"You need a haircut."

Dave smothered a sigh at Sandra's abrupt change in topic. "I've been a little busy. I'll take care of it this weekend."

"You've been back a month."

"Twenty days." He sent a silent dare to contradict his timekeeping. In one day shy of three weeks, he'd shed travel-induced fatigue, finalized full-time employment, moved into an apartment, visited his brother across the state, and combed through the official transcripts generated by his dad's death.

"You should let Bar…Babe do it. She keeps me trimmed right nice." Larry pointed to his high and tight cut with barely enough to comb on top.

Babe? The previous men who entered Sandra's life either used her name or the occasional "sweetie" or "dear." He'd never heard anyone—his dad, uncle, or family friend—use "babe."

"No, thanks." Dave stared at Sandra. Would she blurt out her side of the story? It didn't matter to Dave whether she was a licensed cosmetologist or not. He'd promised in the aftermath of the worst night of their lives to never let her near him with a clipper or scissors again. "I could let it grow another couple of months and look for a re-enactment group. A pair of knee breeches and an eighteenth century style coat and I'd be all set."

"Humph."

"I didn't mean to start a family spat." Larry nodded as the server refilled water glasses all around.

"Don't mind her, Larry. We have a variation of this conversation on a regular basis." A memory of his image in the bathroom mirror after the final Sandra haircut sent a shiver across his shoulders. It wasn't so much for the buzz cut on a young boy—the style made him look bald and feel like a shorn sheep—as for the events a few hours later. He'd never viewed broken air conditioners or hot, still, August nights the same again.

"Good stuff. Water. Think I had a stomach virus or something during the night." Larry consumed a third of his drink.

"Pity you got sick on your vacation day. Did you

manage to work in your yard at all?" Sandra lifted a bite of fried fish to her lips.

"Little. This afternoon." Larry turned his attention to his grilled chicken.

Dave thanked the server when she delivered his meal and then gave closer attention to Larry. The older man's pupils appeared tiny for the moderate room light and both eyes looked cloudy with a touch of red. It could be allergies. It could also be a hangover. On the two or three occasions a year when Sandra drank her way through a gin bottle her eyes looked very similar. Maybe these two would stay friends—even more.

He reached for his water as the first bite of salad greens threatened to stall in his throat. *Sandra with a lover?* His imagination refused to expand enough to include the idea. He asked Larry about his yard and relaxed as the conversation stayed with gardens, weather, and food while he ate.

Larry kept his answers short. He appeared to ponder a few of the simple questions and deferred to Sandra more than necessary.

"We should come here again." Sandra pulled the dessert specials menu closer.

"Prefer to stay closer to home." Larry set his empty glass down and signaled the server for another refill.

"No sense of adventure, this one." She smiled at Larry.

He reached over and patted her arm. "Got any urge to explore faraway places out of my system years ago. I like my routine now."

Dave shrugged at their exchange. A trip downtown didn't qualify as adventure in his mind. If he had a reason, he went. Tonight he'd arranged to meet Enrique at the Central Library to discuss the talks scheduled in local churches supporting the medical mission. This restaurant, five blocks from the library, made it possible to park his car only once instead of twice.

"Darla, at the shop, has a new grandchild." Sandra dipped a French fry in tartar sauce and looked at Dave.

"Good for her."

"I'm not getting any younger, David. Neither are you." She leaned forward. "The clock keeps ticking."

"And patience is a virtue." Dave wore a light smile on his face as stiff and false as a mask. "I'm thinking it would be best to find a wife and discuss children with her first." For the previous year Sandra had mentioned other people's grandchildren at an increasing frequency. And since he'd returned from Guatemala, she'd slipped it into every conversation at least once. "You have a grandniece. Doesn't she deserve a doting great aunt?"

"Nice try, David. It's not the same. And they don't live in the area."

"True." He avoided mentioning Cousin Aaron's wife didn't care for Sandra and would be slow to issue an invitation to visit them in Urbana, Illinois.

"I can't help her with little kids." Larry pushed his plate away. "Betty, my only sister, doesn't have children. Looks like you and your brother will need to handle it."

Dave thought of his brother over in Kansas City. Did Sandra mention grandchildren and hint at finding a girl to marry an equal amount to him? As of last week, when they'd spent time together, Joe worked a full time job as a CPA and a part time music gig. He'd not mentioned a girlfriend. Hard to see how he'd fit one into his schedule. "I'll be sure to mention it to Joe."

"Time." Larry tapped his watch for Sandra's attention before picking up the check for their meals.

"Right. Be careful, David. And stay in touch." Sandra stood and leaned toward him.

The scent of lilac filled his nostrils. He blinked back a tally of the number of bottles of the scent he and Joe gave her over the years. It wasn't their fault she asked for perfume and *Lilac Breeze* happened to be the only one available in a plastic bottle conforming to the prison rules. Not much danger losing contact with Sandra. She made it a habit to leave him voice mails and texts multiple times a day. Heat flashed up his neck as if it could ward off her public kiss on the cheek. They both lived with the fact duty and manners outweighed affection between them by a factor of a thousand…or more. He exhaled relief as she opted for a light tap on his shoulder.

Ten minutes later Dave set his empty glass on the table and picked up the check at the end. He glanced toward the entrance and smiled. Maylee, the girl from the park, advanced toward the hostess and cashier area. He strode quickly toward her, eager to greet her before she sat.

"Compliments on your restaurant choice. May I recommend the Oriental salad with glazed chicken?" He addressed Maylee before stepping up to the cash register.

"You're late. For the menu recommendation." She pulled a flat wallet out of an inside jacket pocket before signaling the cashier. "To go order for Morgan?"

The employee turned away to check a list. "They should be packing it now."

"Long day?" Dave cataloged her gray dress pants and a navy blazer and wondered where she worked. Downtown bulged with managers dressed similar. Could she be an attorney? She definitely carried the air of a professional, educated woman in the confident set of her shoulders. He loitered his gaze on her hair, decided the color matched pecans in sunshine and the short, sculpted style practical. "Wash and go," one of his fellow interns had called a similar cut.

She remained silent, observing every movement as he paid for his meal before releasing a smile that included both eyes and mouth. "My work day is predicted to be longer. At the moment, I'm the designated errand girl. It comes with lack of seniority."

"I know all about being at the bottom of the pyramid. I've accumulated exactly four days of seniority. And you?"

"Months."

"Do you like it? Your career?" He patterned his gaze over her, enjoyed the view, and realized she didn't carry a purse. She didn't even have a tourist pack strapped at her waist, Sandra's choice. *Unique.*

"Love it." Her eyes radiated joy. "It's been my dream job for half my life. Oh, my order's up."

He waited while she handed over cash and accepted change and a large bag with room for half a dozen meal boxes. He reached for the bag and brushed against her hand. *More.* His skin shimmered with excitement. "Allow me. I'll walk you to your car."

"You don't want to."

"Because…?"

"It's in the garage at work. Off Olive."

He lifted the bag and held it beyond her polite

reach. "In that case, I'll walk you part way. I'm headed for the library."

"They have branches closer to Saxon Park. Or did you run far from home last night?"

He glanced at her, glimpsed mischief in her gaze. "The person I'm meeting lives downtown. I moved into an apartment near the park last weekend. Does my explanation meet with your approval?"

"Very much so."

"So tell me, how often should I look for Maylee running in the park?" He carried the bag in one hand and tucked the other hand in his pocket before it reached for her. "Do you have a last name? What's the most important thing I should know at the moment?"

"You're asking questions almost as fast as you run."

"Sorry, but it's only two blocks to Olive. We don't have a lot of time."

"Since you put it concise..." She glanced for traffic. "Last name is Morgan. My intention is to run three, maybe four, times a week. And my co-workers are getting hungry and restless."

"Not my fault. The hungry co-worker part." He checked the light and led by half a step across Olive Street. Another question, too personal for a second brief encounter, circled on his tongue. Private life by definition should remain in control of the person doing the living. For all he knew she could be engaged to a jealous bar bouncer. Or—he glanced at her profile again. A committed relationship didn't quite conform to the bits of personality she'd revealed. "I do believe our paths part here. For now?"

"It was...pleasant."

He extended the bag to her, waited an instant for her to secure it, and then swept his palm under her empty right hand. "Pardon me." He lifted her hand as he bowed over it, brushed his lips across her warm skin. His lungs stalled as lips and fingertips lit with excitement. He forced a blink, a breath, and straightened. "Miss Morgan, it has been a pleasure."

He pivoted away before he gave in to another impulse. During his quick, determined, three block walk to the library he resisted the urge to look over his shoulder.

From the third step in front of the grand old building he turned and gazed down the street. Gone. Out of sight. Which store or office building swallowed her up?

****

Maylee buckled her seat belt and accepted the large coffee from Tom. "Thank you. But…"

"It's not for you."

"Then who?" The fast food restaurant they pulled away from was the final entry on their list. In the previous half hour they'd managed to interview the remaining employees on duty last night and the regular customers on the premises. Maylee knew she operated on caffeine with a side order of stubborn. Adrenaline-fueled excitement ran out hours ago, before the end of the hotline follow-ups. Their late round of pharmacy and restaurant interviews drew on reserves she'd been unaware of until tonight.

"One more stop before we call it a night. Or a morning."

She checked the clock on the dash and nodded. Almost one thirty. She pressed her lips tight as Tom steered their black, unmarked sedan into All Saints Cemetery. "So you want to explain?"

"While you chatted up the regular customers I listened to employee complaints. They aren't exactly warm to their frequent homeless visitors." A moment later he turned parallel to the main street, doused the lights, and lowered the front windows. "Listen."

Traffic. Restless leaves on the hedge inside the fence. A few boisterous insects looking for mates. She swallowed back her questions and listened more intently.

Tom drove forward at a walking pace.

Maylee stared at the darker shape of tombstones in dim light.

"At ten o'clock." Tom activated the spotlight and a figure staggered up from the ground.

In an instant, she exited the car and sprinted toward the fleeing man. "Stop. Police."

The man stumbled to a halt when Tom intersected his path. "Didn't do nothing. Don't know nothing."

"We only want to talk." Tom played his penlight over the unwashed face. "Are you Bill?"

"Who told you my name?" He waved the pack he carried and backed away a step. "I ain't going to no shelter."

"Will you drink our coffee? Answer a few questions?"

"Where?" He looked around as if expecting officers to spring from behind every stone.

"Here. Next to the car." Tom gentled his voice another level.

"Hot coffee?"

"We brought sugar packets too." Maylee aimed her

flashlight at his feet.

Bill squatted down and laughed. "You real, lady?"

"Detective to you." She put all the authority she could find into her voice. Too often their interviewees and half the officers on the force responded skeptical of her rank. In addition to being the youngest detective in the department, genetics gifted her with a face more youthful than her chronological age. Clubs and stores always asked for ID when she ordered alcohol. She reminded herself those same genes might be useful later.

Bill got all serious again, fumbled with his backpack. "I'll drink the coffee."

"And the questions?" Maylee eased toward the car.

"I don't want trouble."

Neither do we. She led the trio to the car and pondered Bill and his choice of spring night accommodations.

Half an hour later, questions asked and answered, they left Bill with Maylee's stash of granola bars and Tom's extra bottle of water.

"Interesting character," Maylee masked a yawn. "I'm almost disappointed he spent last night at Francis Park."

"Past your bedtime?" Tom infused his words with a fatherly tone.

Stay in teacher mode. I've already got parents. Well, one remaining. "I can manage."

"Not sure I can." He sighed. "Here's the plan. Unless Johnson and Clark break this thing open from their half of the hot line tips in the next twenty minutes, we'll take a break. Go home. Grab a nap and a shower. Report back at six thirty."

She glanced at the dashboard clock, did a quick calculation, and nodded. One item would appear on her list in addition to Tom's basics. She'd take a minute and write a note to tuck on a certain windshield. A young man, gallant enough to carry a take-out bag and kiss her hand—she glanced down half expecting to see a toasted lip pattern branded there—deserved to know the name of his upstairs neighbor.

Chapter Three

Larry drew smoke from his freshly lit cigarette deep into his lungs. The warm, tobacco laden air swept across the lining of his mouth and throat. He savored the taste of the familiar chemicals and enjoyed a greater level of alertness. At the far end of the loading dock, he leaned against the building, and pulled out his cell phone.

A driver changed gears in a loaded truck pulling away from the building, disturbing the relative silence at Yates Distributing compound. Larry listened for Sandra to pick up. "Hi, sweetie."

"Lawrence? Is something wrong? Why are you calling now?" She rushed her words together.

"Everything's fine. More than fine." His body felt better, more rested and less painful, than it had in weeks. His early batch of medicine didn't complain today at the addition of his breakfast cereal. "I'm on morning break. Getting a little sunshine and wanted to hear your voice. I miss you."

"You're sweet, Lawrence. I'm running behind this morning. I can't talk long or I'll be late for work."

"It's Friday. Would you like to go out tonight?"

"I'm working late. Darla and I are scheduled to close at nine."

He stared at the ash clinging to the end of his smoke. "I forgot." Unorganized words of apology hesitated at the back of his throat. "Listen. Last night. I'm sorry. I didn't intend to get between you and your son."

She made a little noise he couldn't put a name to.

"I asked to meet him. Then I sat there like a grumpy old man during dinner." He thought back to the bulk of the conversation with Dave. He hadn't contributed much. Maybe he should consider the whole idea a mistake. A man like him, well, a forklift operator and a surgeon didn't exactly move in the same circles.

"You were quiet. I figured your stomach was bothering you."

"Yeah. That flu or virus or whatever upset it. It's better today." He imagined Sandra dressed for work in black jeans and flowered blouse. She liked bright colors and clothes with lots of buttons and zippers. While her co-workers at the salon favored scrub tops in solid colors she shied away from them. And he couldn't fault her for it. He avoided telling her the reason for his stomach problem, the real source of his sickness yesterday. He'd not mentioned his lapse at their AA meeting either. One of these times, on the next visit, he needed to confess his alcoholism to his army buddy. Paul always brought a twelve-pack or two and the memories of when they were twenty-one. Drunk or sober, they planned to rise to the top. It seemed to have worked out a little better for Paul. He managed to work for the same company steady for twenty years. A wife, a house, a real family completed the ideal they'd talked about all those years ago.

"Call me later." He pulled her image forward again, put a smile on her face. Sandra's smile could charm him into doing all those little polite things men should do for the women in their life. She shared so much with Barbara, the girl he almost married years ago. When either girl turned up the corners of her mouth and parted her lips in invitation to laugh he complied. "I'd like a moment when you have a break this afternoon. We can make plans for this weekend."

"Will do. I've got to get going."

"Same here. Take care, Ba…babe." He ended the call and exhaled. *Almost called her Barbara.*

He pocketed the phone and reviewed a few of the unexpected twists in his life. It resembled a roller coaster with all the dips and turns tracing his periods of good, bad, and no employment. His abilities plummeted more than once when the drink gained control. His true love, Barbara, was taken from him years ago. Whiskey stayed his only friend during the worst of it.

"Paid a steep price for having a smooth, liquid, Tennessee friend." He muttered while memories of the mixture of good and dead end jobs plus the year with only sporadic day labor returned. "Still miss you, Barbara. The rest of the world calls it a tragic accident. I know better." He ground out his cigarette against the cinder block wall and pushed upright. "Only agree with the first word. The so-called accident was murder."

A door slammed in the distance, and he popped back to the present. No matter how kind the lady friend of the moment acted, he kept a special place in his heart for Barbara. Sandra's image flitted across his mind and he sighed. She understood better than most. Then again, she kept a closet full of her own secrets.

Larry walked into the employee lunch room with five minutes left on his break. Jim, the other forklift operator, worked a number puzzle while the television ran a morning news show on mute. "What's new?"

"Same rumors as last week. Company's for sale. Mr. Yates refuses to sell. Take your pick." Jim filled in the final number and leaned back wearing a satisfied look.

Larry started to open his mouth with a comment on a rumor the company was closing. "What?" He stared at the TV where a view of All Saints Cemetery filled the screen. He leaned forward and squinted to bring the closed caption into focus. The program cut to a commercial before he could read it all. "What happened in a cemetery to make the news?"

"Where you been hiding? The story's all over the TV last night and this morning. The police found a dead man sprawled out across a grave. Guess they're still trying to ID him. Whole thing's weird if you ask me." Jim went to the sink and dumped the dregs from his coffee cup. "You okay?"

Larry sank onto the nearest chair. The kneeling angel stone so prominent on the screen a minute ago, he knew the place. Barbara rested a few paces away, one row east, next to her grandparents. "Need a minute."

Jim set a paper cup of water in front of him. "Drink this. You turned white. Looked like you'd seen a ghost or something."

Seen a ghost? No, he sighed and nodded thanks to Jim for the water. Today, first thing after work, he needed to drive to the cemetery. He'd take a flower. Check Barbara's resting place. He would do anything necessary to keep her at peace.

****

"Thank you, Sergeant." Maylee ended the call to the head of airport security. One more thing on Tom's list—as if she couldn't have compiled the same items this morning. She made a slight detour for a bottle of water before returning to the interview room. She checked her watch an instant before knocking and opened the door. Six minutes, not bad to arrange welcome and transportation for Luci Saterro.

Tom glanced in her direction as she stepped into the room and set the water in front of Tony.

"As I was saying..." Tony Lorenti leaned back in the simple, heavy chair. A large man and proud of it, he spread his hands wide on the table as if to show off his multiple rings, expensive watch, and gold wrist chain. "My brother-in-law drove a car until it wore out. His German sedan, while nice, hails from 2003. Luci's small SUV isn't much better—two, no, three years younger. Talked to him about it regular, but he could be stubborn. Doc tends to be too thrifty for my taste."

Maylee peered at Tom's notes. The narrative of Tony's visit to the Saterro residence prior to calling in the missing adult report had progressed at possum speed during her absence. The highlights consisted of opening the back door with a spare key, entering the alarm code, and inspecting the garage. She organized a few of her own questions to add when the men's chronology moved into the main portion of the house.

"Did you touch anything aside from the light switch and door handle?" Tom nudged.

"No. Don't think so. I walked a full circuit around each vehicle. On the off chance Art was inside one or the other."

Tom nodded. "After the garage?"

Tony broke the seal on his water. "Is Luci on her way?"

"Arrangements are in place, Mr. Lorenti. Your sister will be escorted here as soon as her flight arrives." Maylee noticed more concern in his eyes at mention of his sister than demonstrated during questions of his missing brother-in-law. Tilt of emotion toward blood relations could be expected. The extent of the difference bothered her. "I believe Detective Wilson asked a question."

"Oh, yes, well, let's see. I called his name a few times. I didn't want to sneak up on him if he happened to be sick in the bathroom or something."

During the next several minutes, Tony took them on a verbal tour of the kitchen, dining, and living rooms. He described classic furnishings in good order with drapes drawn across the large front window.

"Knew something was wrong the moment I pushed open the bedroom door. Bed was in a tangle, sheets all twisted, and doc's pajamas spread out across the lumpy mess. I found a pillow on the floor, where it didn't belong, so I picked it up. Hate clutter and things scattered around." Tony addressed Tom. A moment later he added, "Sorry," as if he'd translated the detective's expression.

"Anything else? Chairs? Lamps?"

"Doc's suitcase was open on a chest at the foot of the bed. It looked packed for his long weekend in Chicago, as far as I could tell. Then I checked the bathroom. Art's scuffed up toiletry case sat on the counter. Only sign of him. I called Luci back right away." He laid his hands flat on the table as if about to stand and end the interview.

"What time did you talk to your sister?" Maylee put a casual note into the serious question.

"Almost midnight. She designated me to call in the report." He slid the water bottle several inches from one hand to the other. "What does it say on your report? Before one this morning?"

"Just for the record"—Maylee studied Tony's large, thick fingers—"which of your cars did you take to the house?"

"The new Cadillac Sport Sedan. You want a ride in it?" He sent the sort of smile men of his generation favored when trying to pick up a companion in a bar. The expression and connotation sent a chill across Maylee's neck.

She maintained her serious, business expression and hid how much she would like to look in his car— with an evidence collection technician. Before she voiced another question, three knocks sounded on the door and Detective Johnson leaned into the room.

"Preliminary report from the M.E."

Medical examiner's prompt today. Maylee sealed her lips with a dab of the patience Tom frequently advised.

"Good timing." Tom rose and accepted a single sheet of paper. He studied it for a moment before handing it to Maylee. "Mr. Lorenti, we'd like to go back in time a little further. When did you last see Dr. Saterro?"

Tony shrugged. "Weekend? Luci took a Sunday morning flight. I stopped by to wish her well on Saturday."

"You spoke with both of them?" She waited for his nod before continuing. "Any memorable topics in your conversation with the doctor? Did you argue?"

"Waste of breath to get into a dispute with him. All

these years and he squeezed every nickel twice. Not necessary. He made good money cutting people open and sewing them back together. He and Luci could have lived well, traveled to Europe."

She added another item to the complaints of the Saterro life style. "Staying with Saturday, what did you talk about?"

"Luci chattered a lot about the wedding. They only have the one kid, Maria. I guess sharing every bit of planning's normal."

"And the doc? What did he talk about?"

Tony took a gulp of water and recapped the bottle. "Showed me an audio book he planned to listen to on the drive. A biography of Pope Francis, I think. Luci and he, they both take their religion more serious than I do."

"Anything else?"

"He mentioned a new surgeon. Hired one of his former students, I think."

"Tell me about Wednesday." Maylee jotted a few words in her notebook.

"Why?"

"Humor me." She faked a smile.

"I worked. May's a busy season for limo service—graduations, proms. All sorts of executives visiting the city need quality transportation."

"And later? Going on toward midnight?" Tom slipped his words in nice and neutral.

Maylee ran her fingertip once more under the definitive statement. *Dental records are 100% match to those provided for Arturo L. Sarterro, MD.*

"I don't understand." Tony started to stand until Tom signaled him back.

"It's a straight question, Mr. Lorenti. Please summarize your activities from Wednesday evening until you walked into your office on Thursday morning." She tucked the single page report into their manila folder and turned to a new page in her small notebook.

"What are you implying? I reported my brother-in-law missing. Luci started to worry when he didn't arrive in Chicago or answer his phone. Have you found him? My sister—"

Tony's jaw froze as the truth hit. "He's dead."

Maylee leaned back, out of the easy circle of Tony's fist, preparing for wild, angry gestures accompanied by a verbal explosion. She focused on his right hand, waited in silence for a twitch, a wiggle, anything to warn of an unleashed temper. The verbal modifiers the man sprinkled into his answers this morning—tightwad, cheap, worn, old—demonstrated Tony Lorenti tolerated rather than admired the late Arturo Saterro.

Tony clenched and released his hands while his face darkened with a sudden rush of blood. A swallow and series of blinks later he settled a narrowed gaze on a bit of wall behind her. "You've got it wrong."

She counted the seconds until he found more words.

"Luci asked me to go over to the house when he didn't show. I reported him missing. I've been patient and cooperative."

Tom picked up the file and tapped it on the table. "Then stay agreeable and talkative. Tell us about Wednesday night into Thursday morning."

"My lawyer will hear about this." Tony crossed his

arms over his chest and glared.

"You're not under arrest." She eased her chair back and gathered up papers as she stood.

He raised his chin to classic schoolyard dare level and quieted his breathing.

Maylee counted three full seconds of silence before Tony spoke.

"I need to be with Luci when you tell her. Then we leave. If you've questions, get a subpoena."

A few moments later, Maylee dropped the file on Tom's workstation and sank into the visitor chair. She plucked a mint from a small dish and began to unwrap it, grateful for Tom's candy stash. The story circulating in the department claimed mints replaced his cigarettes two years ago. She'd not known him when he changed habits, but sometimes the grapevine got things right. "Thank God, he's not my brother."

"Nor mine." Tom tugged two pages of notes off the legal pad, stapled them together, and added it to the folder.

"He missed a question." She twisted the empty wrapper. "Tony never asked where we found Dr. Saterro."

"We'll keep him close. He's family."

"He's our first suspect."

"Exactly. Wilson's maxim. Keep the family close and your suspects closer."

Chapter Four

Dave allowed one small bubble of happy anticipation to cross his face before greeting his next patient. Every break, even the tiny ones today, brought a memory of the note on his windshield this morning. Written in the form of a coupon, it offered "coffee and conversation" and bore a surprise signature—"resident of 202, Maylee Morgan."

This weekend? This evening?

He opened the electronic chart for his next patient and turned his demeanor to professional.

A quarter hour later he offered a brief handshake to his departing patient and tuned into the background noise. The air weighed somber, heavier than during his previous intervals in this space. He scanned the public area, his senses on alert as if an unseen force imposed quiet with a threat. He glanced toward the reception area and didn't see anything unusual. Patients waited for their mid-afternoon appointments by thumbing magazines and ignoring each other.

Stella, a model of quiet efficiency, worked at the sliding window. Half an hour ago, Gloria and her bubbly enthusiasm greeted patients. He didn't remember this much difference when the office assistants changed places yesterday. Could one employee's personality make the difference?

"Dr. Holmes."

He turned toward Dr. DeVino, the senior general surgeon at the clinic today. He wore a subdued expression, complete with a frown line attempting to settle on his forehead. *Can patients read bad news on my face as easily as I see it on his?* "Problem?"

"Nothing you've done. We need to talk about Dr. Art." He stepped further back into the hall, gesturing Dave to follow.

"Okay." Dr. Art Saterro, his mentor and the clinic's chief surgeon, should be in Chicago, enjoying a long weekend with his wife, daughter and her fiancé. Had he or his family been in an accident? Dave tensed for bad news to match DeVino's face.

"Dr. Art—" He drew a deep breath before rushing his next words. "—is dead. Detectives are interviewing all employees. I've scheduled you last, following Catherine. She'll find you when they're ready."

Dead. Detectives. The words hit Dave low in the gut, like a basketball in a careless pass. He leaned against the wall to hide the sudden sag in his knees. All the moisture fled from his mouth, and he moved his tongue around an invisible wad of gauze. "Wait…are you sure?" He observed his current supervisor nod and stared at his toes. "Police? Not a traffic accident." Semi-organized thoughts tumbled from his lips. A door closed, soft voices reminded him of their surroundings. "I…never mind. I'll take a minute. And then…tend my next patient."

Dave used every acting and focusing trick from high school drama class as he met with his next patients. When he found a moment or two out of sight he chewed antacid tablets and drank water to placate the beast stirring in his stomach. His internal creature surfaced around police, Sandra in large doses, and the memories of a specific night twenty-two years ago. The invisible animal had a nickname—Apprehension—bestowed to limit questions from observant people without the need to know his past.

His scheduled patients cooperated by asking questions. He focused on making his answers deliberate, clear, and in layman's terms to keep his mind in the present. With a little concentration he navigated the new software and entered notes and orders into the electronic charts.

An hour later, after sending the final patient of the day on her way, Dave stared at the closed lunchroom door. Police with questions waited behind it. *After Catherine.* He glanced to the plastic surgeon's office door and the nameplate, Dr. Catherine James. He drew a deep breath, fed Apprehension another dose of antacids, and walked to his office. Phone calls needed to be returned.

"Your turn, Dr. Holmes." Dr. James poked her head into his office fifteen minutes later, when he happened to be between calls.

"Thanks, Dr. James." He lifted a water bottle, discovered it empty, and felt his ribs ache with discomfort at the impending interview. "How was it?"

"Painless." She led him toward the reception area and the break room beyond. "It's as easy as drawing blood."

"You do realize opinions vary on that specific procedure." He tried to match her relaxed smile and managed to shed several drops of tension. *Routine questions.* He drew a deep breath and repeated the proverb about thousand mile journeys beginning with one step.

A moment later he knocked twice on the door and pushed it open. Yellow legal pads, one recorder, and several cellophane wrappers lay scattered on the long table. He flicked his gaze away from the inanimate objects and discovered one person, a woman in gray pants and navy jacket, standing at the coffee maker. His lips froze before a greeting escaped.

Her? She works for the police? A detective? Fragile dreams of shared runs, quiet meals, and warm embraces spun during the past two nights vanished. Apprehension, his internal beast, stood at attention in the curve of his stomach, a carved stone gaining weight by the second.

"Have a seat, Dr. Holmes. My partner stepped out for a few minutes but we can get started. Coffee? Water?" Maylee turned and inspected him over the rim of a paper cup.

Detective. Female. Gun. He swallowed back the primal cry climbing his throat. The trifecta of terror stood five feet away. Once upon a time...until Dr. DeVino told him his boss was dead and detectives needed statements, it had been a better than average day. He shook his head before claiming the nearest metal and fiberglass chair. "This"—he gestured to include the entire room—"is an awkward way to learn your occupation."

She settled across from him and picked up the recorder. "If it makes you less nervous, pretend we've never met until this moment."

"It's not you." He found a half-truth. Why couldn't she have turned out to be a lawyer, or a teacher; any profession except a cop. Apprehension, his creature within, sprang into action, ignored the previous dose of antacid, and clawed at his stomach, attempting to dig a hole for escape. Dave lifted his clasped hands from lap to table and focused on his thumbs. *Stay in the present.* "I'm ready to get this behind us."

"Good. We'll begin." She clicked on the recorder and set it between them. Within thirty seconds she identified herself, date, time and place for the official tape. "Please state your full name for the record."

"David Henry Holmes." He won against the urge to race through the words, swallowed dry fear away from his lips, and continued with his address and job title. He roamed his gaze across her face in search of a smile but none appeared. The non-rational slice of his brain wanted her mouth to curve upward, say it was all a mistake. He wanted to step back in time—to when he discovered the coupon for coffee and conversation. Words intended for the next encounter with the pretty neighbor vanished faster than steam left her coffee cup.

A few questions later, she poised her pen on a new line. "When did you last see Dr. Saterro?"

"Wednesday. Evening." He glanced at the recorder and then to a cabinet handle behind her. After the first two questions, he'd discovered when he focused on either her eyes or lips for more than an instant it distracted him from the words. "I went over to his house after…after my…our…the run."

"Because?"

"He invited me. Gave me a gift. A cookbook." He watched her lips press so tight they almost vanished. "What? You don't believe I cook?" He moved his gaze to the trail of combination printing and cursive her pen left across the yellow paper.

The Marshall, Missouri, police detectives used the same type legal pads. Audio recorders were larger twenty-two years ago. He slipped back to the familiar mental memory of a young boy swinging his feet inches above a gray tile floor surrounded by three adult strangers. The man in the white shirt and striped tie asked the questions. He asked the same question with the words in different order over and over as if he didn't believe the first five answers. He'd told Dave the woman was his advocate—whatever that meant—but she smelled of strong perfume and wore a chopstick in her hair. None of them listened when he asked to see his dad.

"Cooking isn't the issue. What time did you leave his place?"

He jerked out of the past. "Pardon me, could you repeat the question?"

"Time. We need the time you left."

"I didn't check my watch." He pulled the image of Dr. Art standing inside his front door forward and held onto it. What were his parting words? Yes, the carpenter's joke about measuring twice before cutting once.

"But?"

"Ten o'clock news came on before I got home." *Why is the time Wednesday important?*

In a blink, his mind switched to memories of a ride through the dark streets in Marshall the night everything changed. Once again he could see his child body plain as an internal video, whispering the lie to his brother Joe everything would be okay. Other images, not as pleasant, lapped at the edge of his mind. This time he fought it off. He was an adult now, equal in size and intellect to the questioner. Today he didn't have the burning need to see his father, to confirm with touch what the images seared into his mind told him.

A soft creak and click at the door announced the entrance of another person. The noise and motion pulled him out of the memory pit before it drowned him. He focused first on Maylee and then the man in a polo shirt. A handgun rested in a holster at his waist, six inches from a pair of handcuffs. Dave's lungs froze and caused his heart to skip a beat. This must be her partner. He forced a swallow and didn't take his gaze away from the new arrival's thick, black belt.

"Continue." The word came out with authority as the second detective skimmed Maylee's notes over her shoulder.

"And was he well? Dr. Saterro?" She slid the new question at Dave.

"Yes."

"What did you talk about?"

"Medical stuff. People we both know. Bits and pieces from my recent Guatemala experience." He shifted in his seat in an effort to slow down Apprehension's running in place. The temptation to walk to the fridge and pour a glass of filtered water caused him to swallow the dry air in his mouth.

"How long to drive home?"

Dave studied his thumbs and hunted for sense in her simple words.

"Other cars?" Her partner broke his silence.

"What?" Dave moved his attention to the man.

"Tell us about traffic in front of the Saterro house. Cars parked along the street." He flipped a wrapped mint in Dave's direction. "My name's Wilson."

He reached for the treat without thinking and occupied his hands with the thin plastic. "I didn't notice any vehicles parked on the street. But I didn't pay attention to the driveways."

"Pedestrians?"

Dave shook his head, remembered they made an audio, not video recording, and replied. "None."

Maylee exchanged a hand signal with her partner.

Dave stared at her hand, memorized the short rounded nails with pale pink polish. Practical. Feminine. He blinked away the final wisp of fantasy, an invitation to share a meal of stew and biscuits.

She tapped her pen against paper and posed the next question. "Do you own any firearms, Dr. Holmes?"

The immediate world blackened from all the edges at the same time. One speck of light remained at the end of his private tunnel. He stared at it, lowered his head, and forced a normal size breath.

****

"Do you own any firearms, Dr. Holmes?"

Maylee stared as Dave's complexion faded to within one shade of his bright white lab coat during long seconds of silence. What now? If he faints and cracks his head on the floor we'll be in paperwork and explanations past our knees. Ah, a bit of color above his collar. She sighed as he tipped forward and rested his forehead against his hands. For a full minute she watched his shoulders reflect slow, even breathing.

"No. Never." Dave's words rose muffled on the rebound from the table top.

Tom reached down beside his chair and set a bottle of water in front of Dave. "Take a minute, or three."

She turned the recorder off and reviewed her notes. By his own admission, Dave visited the victim at the early edge of the estimated time of death. Twice during the preliminary questions he'd appeared to drift off, out of the room to parts unknown. Did he mentally return to the scene of his crime? She skimmed over the facts at hand aside from his address. He ran well, managed to keep long hair clean and confined when not running, and drove an economical car. She could learn almost as much from his driver's license.

He raised his head, settled back in his chair, and opened the water.

"Better?" She detected enough color to confirm humanity, not zombie creature.

"Are you telling me Dr. Art was shot?"

"I'm asking the routine questions for a murder investigation." She stretched the truth. The other clinic employees were character witnesses—not in contact with Dr. Saterro after he left the clinic late Wednesday afternoon. Dave's own words gave him opportunity to commit the crime. He needed to be classified as suspect. Although his reaction hinted he wasn't aware of the method of his boss's death.

He took another swallow of water and turned to Tom Wilson. "Was he shot? It matters."

"We're not releasing the cause of death at this time."

She stared at his grip on the bottle. One more ounce of pressure and the plastic would crumble like foil. He possessed strong hands. Nimble hands. Capable of holding a pillow over nose and mouth firm enough and long enough to kill a man. What of the mind to command the hands? Did it contain the evil intent and will to commit the deed?

She sent a quick, apologetic glance to Tom. "No firearms were involved in Dr. Saterro's death."

She deflected her partner's silent displeasure. The change in Dave's posture and return to cooperative facial expression confirmed her decision to vary from the usual replies.

"Good." Dave recapped the water.

Maylee guided him through questions about his route to and from the Saterro house. She managed to get him to tell her portions of the conversation. Then she asked him for a tour of the house, detailing each room he'd entered, which chair he'd occupied, what he'd touched.

"May I?" Dave pulled a roll of antacids from his shirt pocket and displayed it to them before thumbing off two.

"Stomach problem?" She turned to a new page on her legal pad.

"It comes and goes. Worse today."

She stared into his eyes, searched for lies, but found only confusion. "We're almost done."

A dozen questions later, when Dave exited, Tom closed the door and faced her.

"You want an explanation." Maylee pocketed the recorder. "He lives in the same apartment building, moved in last weekend. We've spoken to each other, briefly, a couple of times."

"That's all?"

She nodded. As she cleared off the table, a mental inventory of their acquaintance scrolled past. First, they met during a run in the park and exchanged a little casual conversation. Yesterday, when they crossed paths at the restaurant, he flirted and walked her half way back to the station. And this morning, very early, she'd left a note on his windshield, her own return flirt. She didn't think even the most particular Police Captain could find conflict of interest in the encounters. "Do you need a detailed list?"

She offered a record of the actual, real life, interactions. The others—the dozens of times the blond runner invaded her nighttime thoughts—needed to be forgotten. The countless times her fingers tingled in desire to touch his pale hair or bare cheek would have to stop.

****

"Deaf." Dave threw the basketball against the backboard.

"Blind." He caught the rebound.

"Dumb. Dumb. Stupid." The ball alternated between the concrete drive and his open hand.

He ignored the warm, early evening air and the subdivision noise of children after school and parents returning from work. For a moment he paused to wipe his sleeve across his brow and then resumed his practice. Therapy would be a better word. After clinic hours he'd fled here, to his childhood home, the house of Uncle Bob and Aunt Joan. *Sanctuary.* Old habits die slow. Apartments provide temporary shelter. Sandra's house made him cautious—the status of a guest uncertain of his welcome.

So far only his body exhibited exhaustion. He charged forward, made a perfect layup as his mind continued to move in dips and swirls worthy of the most complicated rollercoaster.

Dr. Art is dead. Murdered. Never again would

Dave be able to discuss a surgical case with his mentor. The stupid little exchange as he stepped out the door would be…already was…their final conversation. Plans under construction for conferences, papers, and charity work dissolved with the quiet, strained words this afternoon.

Dave blinked away threatening tears and took a shot from the free throw line. The ball swished through the net.

"Good shot."

He turned to see Uncle Bob standing at the end of the drive. His uncle stood in a pose common to the end of a workday, his suit coat hooked over a finger and draped over his left shoulder. "Not many today."

"Have you been at this long?"

"Long enough." He dribbled to occupy his hands. "It's been a rough day."

"At the end of a rough week." Bob opened the door for conversation. "Care to join me out back in a few. We can swap tales of woe over a brew."

"In five." Dave glanced at his watch. He'd give his uncle, one of the most patient men in the world, a few moments of peace before dropping a summary of his afternoon on him. The man who stepped in as father to Dave and Joe twenty-two years ago deserved a little transition time between the cares of a busy auto dealership and listening to Dave's current problem.

Sandra. His next shot rolled around the rim before falling off on the outside. The news today made it difficult not to remember—remember the night her suspicion or impulse boiled over into action. The waves and tremors she stirred in seconds managed to affect all those close to her years later.

Dave shot three more successful free throws before collecting the ball and tossing it into a scarred garbage can to join other sports equipment on his way through the garage.

A few minutes later he handed a local beer to Bob before topping off his sports bottle with lemonade. "Have you paid attention to the news today?"

Bob led them out to a small patio. "Should I? Did we get pulled into war in a jungle somewhere?"

"This is a local story."

"Enlighten me."

Dave settled into a plastic chair and looked out to the bright silver chain link surrounding a patch of lawn, grape arbor, and tilled rectangle waiting for the vegetable garden. "Dr. Art is dead."

Bob set his drink down hard on the small table. "When?"

"Late Wednesday, I think." Dave turned his gaze to his uncle and studied what his own face would look like in thirty years. If he survived until then. "The murder victim found at All Saints. They identified him as Dr. Art. Police aren't saying much about how or when he died."

"When did you find out?"

He glanced at his watch. "Two…closer to three hours ago. Detectives came to the clinic and questioned everyone."

Bob tipped his head back into his deep thinking position. "How did it go for you?"

"Difficult." He sipped lemonade. "I talked to him Wednesday night…at his house…Dr. Art. Police asked sixteen different ways what time I left. I recited every turn on my route home at least half a dozen times. They wanted to know every time I braked plus every car, moving or stationary, in the entire subdivision. I'm ninety-nine point ninety-nine one hundredths percent certain they have suspect written by my name."

"I'm sorry, Dave."

He forced a shrug. "No need for sympathy, unless you killed him."

"No motive." Bob raised his beer. "You want me to retract the apology?"

"I'd like—" He blinked a swirl of half-formed words to a halt. "It's a long list. Top item is the real killer turning himself in."

"Still an optimist, I see."

Dave extended one finger and traced abstract patterns in the condensation of his sports bottle. The negative emotions stirred up by word of Dr. Art's death settled, gave way for a little clarity. Sitting here, with Uncle Bob, gave him the security, safety, and acceptance implied in the word home. "Today's harder than most."

"Have you told Sandra?"

"She sent a couple of texts this afternoon. I haven't figured out a polite reply yet. They have a TV in the shop. She probably recognized the name and will play-act concern. I'm not looking for pity—never from her." Dave gazed out at the yard while portions of Wednesday night replayed like poor quality video in his head.

He could see Dr. Art standing inside the storm door, lifting his hand in farewell. The gift, the companion cookbook to one of his favorite PBS shows sat on the passenger seat. The kind words scrawled on the flyleaf—were they the final ones Dr. Art wrote? "I should have stopped for milk on the way home. Or a candy bar. Anything to get a timed receipt."

"They'll clear you. It might progress slower than we'd like, but our system works better than most."

Dave swallowed a quick phrase of dispute. Sandra gave them all exposure to the criminal justice system the summer he was eight. *Emphasis on criminal.* After the initial hours, at the police station, Dave's part mercifully faded to observer more than participant.

He stood tall and held Joe's hand at the funeral.

The brothers remained on padded benches during a custody hearing months later. They ignored the little puzzles in their hands and focused on lawyers trading papers back and forth to a judge while Bob and his wife, Joan, sat tense at a plain table.

"Meet any of your new neighbors?" Bob cranked the patio umbrella open as the setting sun poked at them between houses.

"Yeah. Met the woman upstairs while running in the park. Wednesday. She's one of the detectives stamping me 'Suspect.'" *Miss Perfect Legs carries a handgun.* Furry little Apprehension awoke and used his stomach for a trampoline.

Chapter Five

Maylee released her seat belt and reached for the passenger door handle in one economical move. Morning sunshine flashed against the moving, tinted glass. "If we get a confession from Dr. Saterro's neighbors, will you let me drive back to headquarters?"

"Don't count on it." Tom eased out of the driver's seat of the black sedan. "Safe money's on neither a confession nor driving."

"A girl can hope." She sent a smile in his direction and watched one side of his mouth twitch upward. If he were a relative instead of her trainer with the power of an evaluation, she'd accuse him of playing a foolish game. She understood he wanted to drive part of the time. And she'd accept it in a minute if he drove most of the time. Instead, he insisted on total possession of the steering wheel since the second week of their partnership.

"It's already May. Do I need to find a witness to your statement of 'one more month' dated the first week of April?"

"Bothers you that much?"

"Only on the days we take out the car." She pushed the heavy door until it closed with a solid thud.

"I let you drive. Twice."

"During my second week as a detective. You do recall I parked legally in front of the witness' house?"

"Absolutely. I also remember what happened thirty seconds later."

"Neither of us could control it." She shook her head, picturing once again the distraught homeowner driving up in a full size van and plowing into the rear of the unmarked cruiser.

The incident generated only slightly less paperwork than the previous time a car assigned to her suffered damage. In the incident three years ago, her patrol car lost a rear window and gained four bullet holes. Not from the suspect they managed to stop with spike strips. No, the officer next to her at the roadblock got nervous, fired his weapon, and hit the cruiser.

"After this case." Tom performed a quick, two-finger salute. "On my honor."

"You always do this with no witnesses." She scanned the block and didn't see anyone outside this early on a Saturday. The lawns stretched neat and trimmed on both sides of the street and the one-story homes looked well maintained. Everything indicated upper-middle-class pride of ownership. To her left, crime scene tape fluttered across the doors of the Saterro house. Directly in front of her stood a mirror twin, the garages separated by a narrow strip of green and the window pattern indicating living and bedroom areas.

She stepped forward, led them up to a small, square porch, and rang the bell. These were the only neighbors not home either time the uniformed officers canvassed along this street yesterday.

"Police officers, we'd like to ask a few questions." Maylee displayed her badge to a slender, blond woman when the door opened.

"It's about Dr. Saterro, isn't it? I don't think we'll be able to help you much. Would you accept coffee?" The woman, dressed in yoga pants and a sleeveless top, gestured them into the house. "My husband's on a tight schedule this morning. We'll have to talk while John eats."

Maylee followed the woman toward the aroma of fresh coffee and a breakfast table in a sunny kitchen. Without a backward glance she remained confident Tom made a mental inventory of floor plan and furnishings. "That's fine. We're used to multi-tasking."

"It's a real shame about the doc. I'm Betty. Betty Fielding. Sit. When will Luci be able to return? They're good neighbors. Luci's so excited about the wedding. Doc planted new roses last week. Wonder what will happen to them." She rambled with questions as she removed a mug from the coffee maker and started another large cup to brew.

"First things first." Maylee opened her notebook. "What is the correct spelling of your name?"

Half a dozen questions later a balding, middle-aged man dressed in a US Postal Service uniform approached from the bedroom portion of the house. He nodded to each of them. "St. Louis' finest in question mode already?"

"Early and often," Tom replied while watching John Fielding pick up his coffee and pull out the final chair at the table.

Maylee took more detailed notes than Tom while they shared almost equally in asking the questions. She declined a second offer of coffee and overlapped her question with Tom's previous query. "Did you look over at the Saterros' on Wednesday when you locked up for the night?"

"Not the easiest view." John brushed toast crumbs from the corner of his mouth. "As I said, we folded our proverbial wings early that night. I think I made the last rounds a few minutes past nine."

"Any cars parked on the street?" Maylee hunted for a third confirmation of Dave's visit. *We need to know when he left.* She stuffed thoughts of her new neighbor away. A crisp memory of his clean-shaven face and enticing wheaten hair began to intrude again. Thoughts of loosening the single band confining his hair above his collar threatened to consume more attention than she could afford while working a case. "Pedestrians?"

"No one walking. I did notice a car parked next door. Small. Orange. Toyota? Not sure about the last. Don't recall seeing it in the neighborhood before." He took another gulp of coffee. "Almost done?"

"One more thing." Maylee looked John full in the face. "Are you aware of anyone having an argument with Dr. Saterro or making threats against him?"

"Not me. We get along fine."

"And the other neighbors? Visitors?" She kept her voice even.

"Larry? My brother-in-law and Doc never meshed." John exchanged a glance and a nod with his wife. "I need to go. Betty can give you details. Neither storm nor police questions and all manner of things."

Tom stood and walked out with John to gain an extra minute and a question or two out of Betty's hearing.

Betty folded a paper napkin into a smaller and smaller square. "Larry's my brother. He…well…he's a little peculiar around Doc, avoids him for the most part."

"Can you be specific?"

"A few weeks ago…I can't remember the date. Larry comes over on Sunday. It's a tradition of sorts— lunch here after mass."

Maylee stilled her pen and focused on Betty's restless fingers.

"Doc was washing cars in his driveway. Guess the hose got out of control, and he sprayed Larry's truck."

Maylee nodded as Tom returned in silence.

Betty took a deep breath and rushed her next words. "The driver's window was down. Larry yelled curses and stormed back in for towels. He refused Doc's offer to help clean up the mess. Ranted on about how all the man's education made him think he was special, on a shelf above the rest of us. John and I both talked to him, but it still took a good ten minutes before he calmed down."

"Is that the only incident you witnessed between them?"

"It's the most recent. Worst. Most of the time Larry ignores Doc." Betty gathered up the breakfast dishes. "Larry refused to go with us once when Luci waved us over for dessert. Made a comment about not breaking bread with a man who had done him harm. I pressed him. Larry clammed up and went home. Neither of us mentioned it the next time we got together."

"What's your brother's full name?"

"Lawrence Thompson. I suppose you'll want address and phone." Betty sighed. "He's not going to like talking to you. If you want to know about comings and goings in his block, ask the elderly man across the street. Mr. Mueller."

Ellen Parker

"When was your brother last here?"

"Sunday. He left earlier than usual. Right after lunch. He implied afternoon plans with his lady friend. He manages to use words but not actually share information."

Maylee focused on the other woman's hands as she emptied the dishwasher. "Did he talk to either of the Saterros?"

"I don't think so." She dropped spoons into a drawer. "I don't know when Doc took Luci to the airport. It's possible they crossed paths. You'll have to ask my brother."

"We will."

****

Maylee selected a table for lunch break by the window in Grand Avenue Hospital cafeteria. Sunshine through the glass warmed her face and banished the chilly attitude of their most recent interviewee. Evidently operating room nurses took confidentiality beyond the letter of the HIPPA law. She glanced out to traffic three stories below and punched in the code for Kate. The Saterro case didn't allow for social outings to International Festivals at this stage.

"Excellent timing, my friend." Kate's voice startled her into rising to her toes after two rings.

"I expected to get voice mail."

"And you get the real me. Lucky girl."

"About tonight." Maylee nodded to Tom as he set down his tray. "I won't be able to join you. Duty calls."

"Poor you. I don't suppose you could beg off? I'm in need of girl talk tonight. Family stuff happened."

"Your mother?"

"No, she's fine. No, wrong word. Healthy. Her

58

brother died unexpectedly. I'm going to be deep into Italian gatherings for the next several days."

"I'm sorry about your uncle." Maylee reviewed the several visits over the years to Kate's maternal home and didn't recall meeting other relatives. Uncles and aunts and cousins had been mentioned in passing but never present.

"Could you do me a favor?" Kate's voice grew strained.

"For you—anything legal."

"Uncle Art, he's one of the city's murder victims. Can you keep me updated? Aunt Luci and the rest of the family are in a tight emotional spiral. Information would be good. An arrest better."

No wonder the relatives seemed familiar when I skimmed the list. She moistened her lips and pulled a professional shield between her and her best friend from the college track team. "You know I can't comment on active investigations."

"Don't blame me for asking."

"It never hurts to ask, Kate. I'll keep you on the list of people to contact when the case is resolved. Meanwhile…" She forced a smile at Tom. "Anything more from your computer friend?"

Kate laughed. "He sent a short little message last night. Did I tell you he's down at Fort Leonard Wood?"

"No, you didn't mention it. Should I have Matt check him out? He could put a little fear of the MPs into him." Matthew, the youngest of the Morgan brothers, currently trained military police at the Missouri army base.

"Not necessary. He's unable to get off this weekend. So the in-person meeting will wait."

"Stalling could be for the good. With all your family turmoil, I mean." Maylee settled into a molded fiberglass chair and poked her fork into the daily special, chicken pot-pie. "By the way, the boys can't decide what to get for mother's yard this year. Could you come up with three or four possibilities? She's out of room for roses. We're thinking shade tree, maybe with a leaf rake on the side."

"We've got some beauties. I'll pull a couple aside and you can bring one of the tribe over with you to inspect."

"Sounds good. Lunch is getting cold. Talk to you later."

"You're giving a leaf rake for Mother's Day?" Tom crumbled crackers into tomato soup.

"It's family tradition to give her plants. A tool started as a joke from the grandsons a couple years ago."

"Did you get your sense of humor from her?"

Maylee considered the question as she chewed a cube of chicken. "Kind of difficult to say. I figure a good portion of it is survival tactics with four older brothers. And Dad practiced the 'work hard, play hard' philosophy of life."

"From my viewpoint, I'd say you picked up on the first part."

"Because I cancelled a 'play date' with friends?" She used air quotes to emphasize the key phrase.

"Among other things." He ate a few bites in silence. "After lunch I want to go upstairs and surprise a friend."

"Anyone I know?"

"Sgt. Kurt Zimmer."

"The firearms instructor? Slight build. Hyperactive until holding a weapon?"

Tom smiled so suddenly soup escaped down his chin. "You're dangerous, Morgan."

"They pay me, both of us, to be observant. What happened?"

"Heart problem." He dabbed his napkin across his chin. "He's up in room 822."

Ten minutes later, Maylee stepped into an elevator ahead of Tom.

"Good afternoon, neighbor." She pivoted with unwritten elevator etiquette until she and Dave stood with their shoulders inches apart and both faced the door. In the next breath, she captured a bit of soap mixed with sea breeze after-shave from his direction.

"It was." He placed his hands on the metal bumper bar behind them.

"Have you been back to the park?" She eased a small smile after the neutral question.

"Does it matter?"

"I'm asking as a neighbor. This isn't official." She turned her head a few degrees in his direction and forced a smile. Officially, Dave remained on the suspect list. Video technicians continued to work through traffic camera footage in an effort to see his rather distinctive car on the route home. She'd intended her question to put him at ease, not tense his hands.

"I'm outnumbered." He nodded toward Tom. "Should I even give you time of day without a lawyer? It's thirteen twenty-six, in case you want to jot it in your notebook."

"I won't take notes." She displayed her hands and turned further toward him.

"And him? You brought your detective witness?"

Tom jabbed a button and the car jerked to a halt between floors.

"Neighbors mentioned your car. It's memorable." She didn't specify any of the four people who noticed it parked in front of the Saterro home failed to observe it leave. She held a breath, fighting the increasing weight in her heart each hour they hadn't cleared him. Why didn't she look out her window more often Wednesday evening? She could have taken a break between chapters in the William Clark biography.

"Are you taking me off your list?"

"Not yet."

"Then don't expect me to be chatty." He crossed his arms over his chest; the embroidered name "Dr. David Holmes" visible in black above his hand.

"Tell me about your car. As a friend." *It looks like a difficult vehicle for transporting a body unless you can stand a corpse in close quarters.* She made a mental note to re-check the cargo area dimensions.

"I wanted economical. My uncle is in the auto business. He saved this hybrid for me when the original buyer backed out of the deal. Or were you concerned about the color? The manufacturer calls it habanero."

She glanced to Tom and understood his silent advice to be cautious. "Is it Japanese for orange?"

His lips twitched as if resisting the urge to smile. "I see logic there. But I can neither confirm nor deny your conclusion. My second language is Spanish with Mayan seasoning."

"Have you used it recently?"

"Are you going to claim you didn't check my passport and travel history?"

She tucked her hands into her jacket pockets before they could disobey her brain and touch him. Desire for details of his life not related to the case threatened to invade the conversation. "We ran a very thorough background. On you and the other suspects."

"Then take me off your list and concentrate on someone with motive. And before you ask, no, I don't have names to give you."

The soft, rhythmic delivery of his words tipped her internal lie detector into the truth zone. She stared at his face as she lifted her arm and pushed her fingers through her hair. Her jacket rose with the movement, exposing the bottom of Angel's holster.

He blinked, swallowed hard enough to send his Adam's apple into motion.

"Is something wrong?" She watched him struggle on the threshold between expected reply and too much information.

"No." He pointed at the control panel. "They'll be calling maintenance soon."

She widened her stance. "We should talk. As neighbors. First opportunity."

"Catch a killer, and I'll consider it." Dave tapped the button for seven. "Let me expand the statement. Arrest the murderer, and I'll cook you supper."

After Dave's exit, Maylee shrugged to Tom. "No explanation. Gut feeling he's not capable of the murder."

Chapter Six

Dave transferred his gaze from the dining room window to Larry and then to Sandra. Forty-five minutes ago, the couple arrived unannounced and interrupted his quiet Sunday afternoon reading. On the positive side, they'd brought coconut cream pie from his mother's favorite bakery. "Joe didn't give any hints during my recent visit of his next drive to St. Louis. Memorial Day's close enough, I'd expect it to be mentioned."

"He gets three days off from his accounting job." She pressed her fork against stoneware to capture a crumb of crust.

Dave traced the bright pink poppy in the center of the empty plate with his fork. The bites of pie sat in his stomach like a collection of snowballs. If his mother talked much longer, his nervous companion, Apprehension, would start to juggle them. "You're forgetting the music gig. Kansas City kicks off a summer park concert series on the holiday weekend."

"He's neglecting his mother. I've not seen him since the middle of March."

"Not my problem. Any complaints with Joe need to be filed direct with him." Dave stood and began to gather dirty dishes. "My brother is an adult, capable of handling his own schedule. From what I observed a few weeks ago he's built a rather full life."

"Without a girl." She sighed. "He—both of you—

could use a good woman in your life. Where did Angie move?"

Leave it to Sandra to bring up Angie—a med school classmate and family practitioner. Two years ago he'd built a fantasy of them together. But they drifted apart and by the time he wrote his surgical board exams and left for his mission obligation, their relationship dwindled to friendship rather than romance. Angie ended up with a small group practice in a tiny Southwest Missouri town. "West Pine. I'll be attending her wedding in August."

Larry chuckled. "Not as the groom, I suspect."

Dave leaned over to collect the final glass. "Strictly as a guest. Praying she doesn't try to fix me up with one of the bridesmaids."

"Would a date be so bad?" Sandra stood and gestured to the room with her empty mug. "What happened to your furnishings, David?"

"What you see is what I have. Or rather, what I could find last week at the thrift shops." He rinsed a plate and placed it in the dishwasher. The tables, bookcases, and vinyl couch looked older than his thirty years. The floor lamp, a discard from Aunt Joan, went back nearly forty.

"In your last apartment," Sandra narrowed her entire face and stared at him, "the chairs matched."

"They belonged to my roommate. I pretty much culled things down to bed, mattress, and books to store after graduation. No sense in taking up more room than necessary at Uncle Bob's."

"Why did you accept a scholarship with a full page of conditions?"

He shrugged. From the moment Sandra heard

about the requirement to work a charity assignment she'd tossed tiny darts against his shell of resolve. "It worked out well. Medical school is expensive. I applied for as many grants and scholarships as possible. I still have loans to pay."

"Even after they sent you out of the country for a year?"

"Nine months."

"Felt longer to me."

He turned away from her to gather a little patience. It would most likely be a waste of good air but he started to explain again. "They took care of thirty thousand of my tuition in exchange for those months of work. The experience of living in Guatemala, treating diseases and performing surgeries every week, you see maybe once in a lifetime in St. Louis. No one can put a price on educational adventures."

"Now, Sandra." Larry pushed back from the table and put enough soothing into the two words to calm a snarling guard dog. "Leave him be. It's done. He's here. Give him a little time and room to hit his stride. Next time we drop in, the girls will be lined up at the door."

"Selling Girl Scout cookies?" Dave laughed at the image. Did he have an ally in Larry? Had Sandra finally found a man with enough skill to herd her in the direction of peaceful family relations?

"Save me a package of the mints." Larry sent Dave a wink.

"Will do." Today's visit improved his opinion of Sandra's quiet companion. Larry's eyes were clear this afternoon. Whether it had been lack of sleep or hangover or seasonal allergies which Dave noticed with his trained eye a few days ago, it was gone today.

"You haven't answered my question." Sandra walked over and set her mug in the sink.

"Which one?"

"What sort of housewarming gift to buy. I want to get you something for the apartment. After all, it's the first time you're completely on your own, without a roommate. But—" She gestured to include the living room. A worn desk held an array of new laptop and small electronics and a small, thin screen TV perched on top of a full bookcase. Lots of bare wall and floor space remained around the out of style couch. "I don't know where to start."

"Surprise me." He hated suggesting gifts to Sandra. It reminded him of a small child asking for a birthday or Christmas gift. And it highlighted the empty spaces in their relationship.

"Which way does this window face?" Larry brushed one hand across the mini-blinds.

Dave hesitated and double-checked his internal city map. "West. Why?"

"Maybe..." Larry waited for Sandra's full attention. "You could get him a plant. West side of my house has several things doing well. Afternoon light can get hot around here. We should ask around to find a houseplant that will thrive."

"Oh, what a great idea." She stepped over and caressed his cheek. "Will you take me to the same garden center where I got my annuals last week? You should see the place, David. Hanging baskets with ivy draped down making you duck your head the length of the greenhouses. Such a delicious smell. Dirt and blooms and...I'm sorry. Got a little carried away."

Again. He found it difficult to blame her when it came to gardens. She lived too many years without more than a few patches of dull grass for plant life. Sandra loved gardens and flowers. Even at the age of eight, before his family's world changed, he'd been aware she enjoyed plants. The house in Marshall had flowers planted around the front steps and tomatoes and peppers on the sunny side of the garage. And lilacs—he swallowed back a comment as a puff of Sandra's perfume tickled his nose.

"Guess we've settled on a gift." Dave leaned against the counter, crossed his arms, and hoped Sandra got the hint to leave. He had hospital rounds to make.

"Let's go, Sandra." Larry touched her elbow and took a step toward the door.

Good man. "I'll walk you out." Dave doubled down on the suggestion.

"It's a tragedy about your boss, David. You praised Dr. Saterro more than your other instructors. Have they made the funeral arrangements?" Sandra brought up the topic he least wanted to dwell on for another round. He suspected it was the fifth time this afternoon, but he could have lost count.

"It's too soon to know. I'm sure Luci will keep Dr. DeVino informed." Dave expanded to placate Sandra's skeptical look. Funerals. He hated them. Aside from his grandparents, he could count on one hand the number he'd attended since his father's. Dr. Art's service would draw large numbers from the neighborhood and professional circles. After all, an entire career, including published articles, years of teaching, and activity in his neighborhood Catholic parish would be celebrated. Dave's absence wouldn't be noticed.

"Be sure to tell me. I'll send a card."

You and half the city. Dave nodded. A moment later he took a quick step back as Maylee pulled into the lot and parked. A sigh escaped. No way to avoid at least a brief encounter with his neighbor. A little more than twenty-four hours since the incident in the elevator and his gun-toting neighbor poked into his life again. He welcomed her smile and shivered at the thought of her deadly weapon. One quick glance at Sandra and he mentally prepared to make introductions.

"Good evening." Maylee called out over the top of Dave's vehicle before shutting her driver's door.

Dave gave a silent promise to a bouncing Apprehension for antacid tablets in a minute or two as he waved her over. "Sandra, this is my upstairs neighbor. Maylee, meet my mother. And her friend, Larry."

"So pleased to meet you." Sandra extended her hand and ignored the men on either side. "I do so want David to get acquainted with people in the building. He works too much. Grand Avenue Hospital."

Dave looked past the women's brief handshake and studied Larry. The man stood wilted to three shades paler than when they'd stepped outside. The physician part of him went into action, and he stepped closer in case the older man collapsed. What caused it? Did Larry know Maylee's occupation? Was he evading a warrant? He never asked Sandra's friends about their relationship with the police. It wasn't his place to screen the companions of a convicted felon. "You okay? Need water? Place to sit?"

"I'll…be…fine." Larry's voice carried a heavy sandpaper texture.

Dave remained at his elbow, glanced at Sandra and confirmed she remained focused on her own conversation.

"Come on, Sandra. I remembered an errand." Larry straightened as if finding a bit of inner strength and tapped his foot.

"In a minute." Sandra inspected Maylee for a long moment. She must have found her satisfactory for she nodded at Dave and attempted a wink.

Don't go there. He set a hand on Sandra's shoulder and eased her away.

"Nice to meet you. Don't have time to chat. Maybe another day?" Maylee found a comment to cut short Sandra's dive into a detailed conversation.

"Of course. Young people, you're always doing half a dozen things at the same time." Sandra nodded and appeared to get the hint to leave.

A few steps toward the street Dave relaxed his touch on both of them. "Look out for each other. Okay?"

Larry nodded, tugged on Sandra's elbow.

Dave glanced over his shoulder and caught Maylee staring at their awkward tableau. Was she considering a question? He hoped it would wait. If she wanted to arrest Larry for an outstanding warrant, it would be best out of Sandra's sight.

Dave adjusted his stride to match Larry's deliberate steps and directed his words to Sandra. "Don't go getting any ideas."

"Now what makes you say such a thing?" Sandra looked up at him with fake innocence. "She didn't wear any rings. You'd make a nice looking couple. She's a good height for you and your coloring compliments each other. I wonder…do you think I should try a brunette close to her color next time?"

"It's your hair." He glanced again toward the back door where Maylee went out of sight less than a minute ago. If forced to explain the chance meeting in the parking lot, he'd stay with the truth. He neither understood nor controlled his mother—or her friends.

"I'll think about it. Call me." She settled in the passenger seat and reached for the belt.

"Take care." Dave looked at Larry and stared for a long moment at his knuckle-white grip on the wheel. "You safe to drive?"

"I got it, Doc." Larry nodded and started the truck.

Dave stood on the narrow strip of grass between street and sidewalk until the small red and silver truck turned out of sight a block away. *Hospital rounds.* He formed a silent wish for patients and staff to be rational. If not, he'd be shooting baskets at Uncle Bob's past dark.

A few minutes later he hesitated outside his apartment, glanced up the steps and addressed her feet as the owner of the best legs in St. Louis came into view. "Any arrest?"

****

"Not yet." Maylee continued to the bottom step. Her hand tightened on the grocery bag until her nails dug into the palm. A smile evaded her so she settled for a neutral expression. Maybe she should have waited another minute, taken a drink of water, cleaned Angel, anything to occupy a few more moments before heading for her mother's house.

"Sandra will be disappointed."

"Not you?"

"Do I want you to make an arrest? Absolutely. First preference is for the correct man."

She found a tiny smile to send toward him. "We agree on the goal." She studied his face, concentrated on his eyes. She labeled the emotions on their surface as honest confusion and hesitation. Before she could be accused of impolite staring, she blinked and moved her gaze away. "Does your mother come over often?"

"I hope not." He looked at the floor. "Oops. Sandra wanted to see the apartment. I think I disappointed her. Again."

Disappointed by a son who took a straight line from high school to pre-med to medical school and then intern and resident programs plus an overseas mission? Any sane parent she'd ever heard of would be carrying photos in wallet and flashing proud titles at faint opportunities. Her own parents had celebrated all graduations and first jobs in style—backyard parties or fine restaurant dinners.

And Maylee's first impression of Sandra's emotions included forced cheerfulness and obliviousness to Larry's reaction. Not a hint of disappointment.

"Don't worry about it." He pushed back hair which had escaped from its binding and rested on his collar. "Sandra's the outlier of the family. It's a long story. Too complicated for today."

"Right." She skimmed her gaze from his face to shoes and back again. One long lock of hair insisted on staying in front of his ear and taunting her fingers to test the texture. This would never do. Questions raced up her throat, wrestled on her tongue for only an instant before escaping. "Mr. Thom…Larry. Where does he fit into the family?"

"Outside looking in."

Thank you for not mentioning my name stumble. She pushed open the door. "Until next time."

"Detective. I want off your list."

"We're working on it." She waved and stepped outside. Her sigh mixed with the swish of the closing door.

Maylee arrived in Dianne Morgan's backyard twenty minutes later. "Hi, Mom. Your dishes are returned safe and washed."

"I was starting to wonder if you'd make it." Dianne turned her attention away from her newest daughter-in-law, Jennifer, and gave her youngest child a quick hug. "Busy week? Anything you can share?"

"I'm late due to work." Maylee waved at her brothers playing three corner catch with a softball. "Where is…? What?" She suppressed the rest of the question as her two nephews raced out of the house toward the soccer ball. Their mother walked behind and approached the other ladies shaking her head.

"Boys for rent. Cheap. Maylee, isn't it your turn?" Michelle Morgan sank into the final empty lawn chair.

"No thanks. I work with overgrown ones. Remember?" She took a second inventory of the family present. Sunday evening with Mom was a Morgan tradition. Three years ago, after the sudden death of their dad, the children started to drop in, get a little face time with each other as well as their mother, and share dessert. Week by week and month by month it became an integral part of their lives. She drew strength from it and a renewal of her identity. "Matt didn't make it?"

"He's on duty tonight. I'm not sure exactly what it

entails." Dianne pointed to the lemonade pitcher and glasses.

Maylee nodded. Matt, her youngest brother, trained military police at Fort Leonard Wood. Every few weekends he needed to either stay on base or close enough he couldn't make the one hundred plus mile drive to St. Louis.

"Did you have supper? All the fixings for a chicken wrap are in the kitchen." Dianne spoke to her daughter.

"I'm fine." She resolved again to improve her diet. Quick meals during work ended up heavy on calories and light on nutrition. The doctor would not approve. She glanced down, feeling her neck warm at the image of the first doctor who came to mind. He stood an even six foot, exactly right for her five eleven. His blond hair could be elegant when confined or wild and barbaric when running. She shivered at the memory of his blue eyes full of secrets. *He's a suspect.* She needed a replacement fantasy.

She tuned into the conversation of the other three women. They discussed summer plans for the next ten minutes or more. Comments about vacation requests, the high cost of hotels, and the pros and cons of a road trip with children dipped in and out of the talk.

Maylee relaxed for a moment and the encounter in the parking lot returned. Sandra's smile appeared a little forced but became more relaxed in the minute they stood there. Thompson, Larry, made his feelings plain. He wanted away from Maylee. Exactly like yesterday morning, when she and Tom questioned him in his front yard. Mr. Thompson didn't want to volunteer any information.

"What do you think, Maylee?" Dianne leaned over

and tapped her daughter's knee.

"About what?"

"What's his name?" Michelle saluted her with a glass of lemonade.

"Uh…what makes you think I would space out about a guy?" She took a big swallow of her own cold drink.

"It's either a male or a criminal. Or a male criminal," Michelle replied. "I'm trying to put the best face on it."

"A lot of the criminals I meet are male." She grinned at her most outspoken sister-in-law. "New neighbor, too. But he's off limits."

"Married? Spoken for?" Jennifer tossed out two of the common situations where Morgan family values forbid more than casual friendships.

Maylee pressed her lips tight behind her plastic tumbler before "suspect" escaped.

"Regardless of new male neighbors"—Dianne clapped her hands—"I'll uncover the dessert and see if we collect flies or men faster."

Maylee's tension flowed away in the following laughter. Family, her biological one, accepted her all the way to the marrow of her bones. They supplied a safety net to all of their members, regardless of age, occupation, or ability to cook.

"How's my favorite sister?" Steve, her oldest brother, poured a large glass of lemonade before claiming a portion of lawn near his wife.

"Your only female sibling is well." Maylee leaned forward and captured a running nephew before he could jump on his grandmother's lap. "You're speeding, Tyler, going at least twenty in a ten zone."

"No radar gun. Can't prove it." He encircled her neck and gave her cheek a noisy kiss.

"I'll let you off with a warning." She finished the standard exchange and patted her lap in an invitation to sit.

Tyler perched on her knees and started to pull out tiny cars from his pockets.

"I saw you on tape the other day." Steve motioned his older son to sit beside him while directing his words to Maylee.

She shrugged, half expecting the topic to surface between them. He worked as news video editor at one of the nationally affiliated television stations in town. A satellite van from his station had been one of half a dozen media outlets at the cemetery before she and Tom left the scene. "Thank you for not being obvious at All Saints."

"Actually, I didn't go on site. I happened to catch you on the raw footage."

"Did you edit me out? At least show my best side? I haven't taken time to critique the newscasts."

"You have a better side?" He ducked at the invisible object she tossed in his direction. "Final cut featured more tombstones and fence than live people. Why would someone do such a thing? Dump a body on top of an old grave."

"Glad to see we agree on at least one question." She pointed to his hand. "No beer? Have you gone on a diet?"

"Allergy meds." He saluted her with his glass. "New kind this year. It's not pretty when I add alcohol."

"Daddy put the sugar in the fridge." Tyler's

attempted whisper came out loud and clear.

"Among other things," Steve admitted.

"His keeper"—Michelle ruffled her husband's dark hair—"decided he wasn't safe. He even got out of bed one night and started dragging out lumber and tools in the garage."

"We agreed the doghouse needs a new roof."

"At three in the morning?" She gave her husband the light swat aside the head he deserved. "We'd scheduled it for the weekend."

Steve flashed a smile to Michelle and then turned to Maylee. "I've reformed until the prescription runs out or the oak trees stop shedding pollen."

"My wager's on you running out of drugs first." She added allergy meds as the next excuse for memory loss to an already long list used by witnesses or suspects.

"Speaking of wagers..." Dianne claimed the conversational lead. "What side bets do my children have going on for the annual outing to the Memorial Day weekend baseball game?"

Maylee sighed. Another item on the long list of Morgan traditions was to attend the Cardinals game on the Saturday nearest Memorial Day. For the previous three years, she'd lost the friendly wager with her brothers and ended up paying for all the food and drink during the game. The sum tended to grow considerably each year, and she wasn't looking forward to the total this year. "Andrew, Matt, and I need to bring a guest. Same rules as last year."

"My guest is all arranged." Andrew winked at his sister.

"Lucky you." She darted her tongue out at him

before she remembered the nephews were watching. The boys picked up mannerisms, especially the negative ones, faster than traffic cameras captured license plate numbers. Finding a guest should be easy. The criteria merely stipulated an eligible person of the opposite sex. Certainly her luck would change. Or Matt's date would back out at the last minute and they could share expenses. "I've plenty of time."

Nineteen days. She maintained her relaxed smile while her mind scrolled through a very short list of non-cops who met the requirements.

****

Larry avoided more than a momentary glance in Sandra's direction as he drove away from Dave's apartment. The five-mile route to her rented duplex stretched with time and tension until his nerves resembled a spider web hanging on tight in the wind.

"What happened, Lawrence?"

"Personal. Headache came on."

Sandra snorted. "Only time a headache hits within seconds is from a blow to the head."

Or see Detective Ms. Question again. He pulled into Sandra's driveway and turned off the truck. The truth wouldn't do. The moment he mentioned the young woman's occupation or where he'd met her, Sandra would assault him with more questions. How did he know? Why did detectives question him yesterday? Who's Paul? Why did he step off the wagon and into a puddle of booze on Wednesday? "I said it was private."

"You're getting too many headaches. What did your doctor say last time?"

"He changed the dosage on one of my meds."

"You're starting to carry a regular portable

pharmacy. Do you want my opinion?"

He moved his gaze off her face. Her pretty blue eyes saw too much at times like this. His skin warmed under his sport shirt as if she looked past clothing all the way to his internal organs. "Do I have a choice?"

"Next doctor visit, take your sister along. And all of your pills, every last one of them, even those over the counter supplements you bragged about last month." She opened the door and hurried to stand outside. "I'll be taking myself to the garden shop. And the meeting Tuesday. If you come to your senses, we can have dessert after."

Larry shuddered as the truck door slammed. He wanted to follow her, explain. But the fear of her questions won the skirmish, and he waited with forming tears as she unlocked the door and disappeared into her home. *Come to my senses.* He muttered to the empty cab as he backed out and drove away. "Most sensible thing I've done today is walk away from a nosy detective and her questions."

For the remainder of the fifteen-minute drive to his modest brick house he made a dozen attempts to remember the answers he'd given the police yesterday. The questions returned in a rush. When did you last see Dr. Saterro? How would you describe your relationship with him? Where were you Wednesday night? Early Thursday morning? Have you ever been to All Saints cemetery? When did you last visit?

"Dr. Saterro." He spit the name down his front steps as he sat on the porch. It wouldn't be fair to blame Betty and John for moving in next door to the man. A person doesn't really get to pick their neighbors. So he'd cut his visits down to Sundays after mass and special occasions. He avoided his sister's neighbor when possible. The newspaper went on for half a column listing all sorts of good things about the late doctor. They missed an important event. "Damn. Wish I could remember what happened after Paul left."

Closing his eyes, he summoned an image of Paul, his army buddy from Indianapolis, getting into the cab after dark on Wednesday. He remembered going back in the kitchen, putting empty beer bottles in the recycle bag, and…No memory formed.

He shivered in sunshine and let his mind drift to All Saints. Barbara rested there. He'd checked after work on Friday and confirmed the worst. Trampled grass, scraps of yellow police tape, and cigarette butts at the edge of the narrow road announced recent intruders at the Galati family plot. He'd walked to Barbara's flat stone, left a single red rose, and spoken an apology for all the recent trespassers.

Barbara should be here. Sitting beside me. He reached for his pack of cigarettes, found an empty pocket, and remembered he'd smoked the last of today's allotment before they arrived at Dave's.

A few minutes later, Larry picked up Barbara's photograph from the bookcase. "You were the best thing in my life, sweetie. The reckless man who took you from me has paid. They found him desecrating your new home. I'm sorry if he disturbed you."

He settled into a worn leather recliner with a fresh smoke and reflected on the years since the careless driver slammed into the side of Barbara's car. His world changed in one night—with her last breath in Intensive Care. The next morning, a national tragedy stole the attention. Her parents shut him out. They ignored his wishes to follow up and make sure her murderer received justice. Lawyers said he had "no standing." The solitaire diamond ring intended for Barbara's finger, waiting for a final payment at the jewelers, mattered only to him.

"Damn lawyers. Selfish parents. Murdering drivers." He levered out of the chair as his words seeped into the corners of the empty house.

The months following Barbara's death mashed together in his memory. He couldn't put exact times to things anymore. Whiskey helped him forget the insults from her parents and the shunning from the legal system. Somewhere along the line he lost his job. Found another with less pay. Months, almost a year later, he moved out of the apartment in Maplewood and back home with his widowed mother. He recalled a bad year when all he could find were day labor jobs. Sober or drunk it didn't seem to matter. Part of him died with Barbara.

Larry pulled a can of his favorite soda, heavy with both caffeine and sugar, out of the fridge. A moment later, he took his evening medicines, alternating pills with sips of sweet, carbonated beverage. Life went on. He needed to pull his mental state tighter together. If he didn't—he'd lose Sandra. She was the best woman he'd found since Sainted Barbara. She kept her own secrets. Respected his—usually—except today.

Sandra. She didn't even notice at first. Her son did. He stepped beside him quick. He thought he scared him, almost fainted. *Felt close for a moment.* He shook his head, grabbed another can of soda, and headed into the spare room to write a letter.

Chapter Seven

Maylee tapped a name into her computer. "Yes, ma'am, I have it. Luciana Maria Saterro, sole beneficiary. I'm also interested if you have any other policies. Should I repeat the social for you?"

The homicide detective workroom hummed around her. Phone conversations reached her muted by fabric-covered dividers five feet tall. Notes, diagrams, and pictures related to the Saterro case covered all of the surfaces within easy reach. Tony Lorenti, Larry Thompson, and Dave Holmes stared at her from enlargements of their DMV photos. Colored yarn stretched between pushpins connecting several different pieces of paper.

She added information to the open computer file and ended the call with the third insurance company of the day. Dr. Saterro's planning for the future included providing for his family. Luci, the new widow, would receive all the assets they'd uncovered except one small insurance policy designated to Maria, the adult daughter. The previous hour confirmed information rather than offering any surprises or leads. Perhaps when their copy of the will arrived they could find motive.

A mint dropped on her mouse pad.

"Yikes. You get the stealth award for the day." She gestured Tom into her visitor's chair.

"It's the shoes. And the carpet squares." He extended a grainy image of a license plate. "You may remove the surgeon from your display. I'm giving you official permission to flirt with your single, educated, and handsome neighbor."

At least, he said it with a smile. She studied the photo's day, time, and location stamp. Wednesday at 21:47, ten blocks from the Saterro home, the site of the murder. She counted three seconds before she looked up at her partner and sent a silent plea heavenward. Had the delay minimized her blush? "Good to know I don't share a building with a murder suspect. We keep crossing paths without trying."

"Such as?"

"Yesterday. I stopped at the apartment for…it's not important."

"Pause. Rewind. Tell the whole story. I'll toss out the unnecessary bits later." He straightened into interview posture.

She stood, removed Dave's photo from the suspect display and laid it on top of a folder holding transcripts of selected interviews. She looked at the eyes a fraction of a second too long, tucked the photo out of sight, and turned back to her official trainer.

"When I left the station, I stopped at home. I intended to pick up dishes belonging to my mother. Almost before I parked the car, Dave and an older…middle-aged couple, came outside. He introduced the woman to me as his mother. The man—" She reached up and tapped Larry's photo. "Dave gave him the status of his mother's 'friend.' An instant later, Thompson turned pale as copy paper and stammered nonsense about an urgent errand."

"Overt distaste for police is consistent with his behavior on Saturday. Any witness statements tying Thompson and Holmes together prior to yesterday?"

She shook her head and added another thread to chase on her task list. "Yes, Thompson's reaction was almost expected. No tie between them on either background check. And I'd still like to find a reason to get inside Thompson's house."

"No cause."

"Therefore, no warrant request. Yet." She unwrapped a mint and popped it into her mouth. "Dave and his mother, their interactions impressed me as strained...formal. A few minutes later, after the parking lot, I found him loitering in the hall. When I tried to make conversation by asking if his mother came over often, his first response was 'I hope not.' Not at all what I expected."

"Did you get her name?"

"Sandra." She opened the folder with Dave's criminal background check. "He's never used her as an emergency contact. Consistently lists Robert Kale. Affton address."

"Have you run her name?"

Maylee nodded. "Requested twenty minutes ago. Expect the results to come across any moment now."

"One minute." Tom held up a single finger as his phone chimed. "This is Wilson. Good. Looking forward to it."

Business call. She read the information from Tom's face as clear as if he'd spoken. Patience, she reminded herself. It remained one of the virtues she needed to develop. She thumbed through a short stack of files and pulled out the one for Rosa Allegro. At times like this she suspected St. Louis citizens ignored the six degrees of separation touted in sociology papers and went directly to a lower number. Perhaps two.

Tom lowered his phone. "Johnson arrived safe and sound in Indianapolis. He and one local are heading out to interview Paul Michaels now."

"Hope sprouts like a garden seed for the friend to remember Wednesday night better than Thompson." She sighed at the memory of the conversation turning into a confrontation on a small front lawn. Thompson admitted drinking his share of a twelve-pack while eating a take-out supper and reminiscing with his army buddy. He denied any memory past putting his friend in a cab back to his hotel. No time. No name for the cab company. A shrug when asked if he left the house before sunrise.

"Which one is this?" Tom pointed to the file in her hand.

"Family interviews, specifically Luci's sister, Rosa Allegro. You may as well hear this up front from me." She took a deep breath and infused it with all professional tone she contained. "I've met this lady. I've been in her home. Her daughter and I became good friends during college. I've stayed close with the daughter but haven't seen the mother for a year. I hope you don't see this as a problem."

"Continue."

"Officer Hill of District Two patrol interviewed the mother Friday afternoon. Allow me to quote. 'Tony lives large. Makes money and promptly spends it. Luci and Art lived below their means. They bought quality and used it until worn out. They've lived in the same house for thirty years. Once their daughter reached her teens, they spent family vacations working at charity medical clinics.' This doesn't read like motive for murder by Tony. Also, he's not named beneficiary on any insurance policy or bank account which we've found."

"I understand." Tom scanned the remaining portions of the interview. "I didn't like my brother-in-law either. Always figured my sister could have done better. But I waited it out. My wife and I supported her when she admitted he wasn't going to change and filed for divorce."

"Italian. Catholic. Wrong generation for divorce. Anyway, Rosa describes Luci as happy, full of plans for the wedding in September and retirement in a few years. Her financials support the assessment with lack of spending sprees or places where the victim cancelled her credit cards." Maylee accepted the file and returned it to the collection of interviews.

"We're back to Thompson."

"Or one of the lawsuit plaintiffs." She swept her gaze over another grouping of photos pinned to her wall. These men had filed lawsuits against Dr. Saterro, Grand Avenue Surgical Clinic, or the surgery department of Grand Avenue Hospital. All three cases moved through the legal system at an uneven pace toward out-of-court settlements. The office correspondence lacked any recent threatening letters or notations of phone calls indicating a distraught family member with motive or opportunity to bypass the legal system.

Tom shook his head and reclaimed the traffic camera photos. "Keep Tony on the list. This murder was too personal. A decorative pillow held against the victim's face. Signs the victim roused enough to struggle. So I'm thinking a man. Not a lot of women would have the strength to complete it."

"I agree." Maylee reviewed the master list of interviewees. She paused her finger at Mueller, Thompson's observant, night-owl neighbor. The man had lived in the same house forever. During the Saturday interview he wanted to talk about Thompson's mother as much as anyone. "Do you remember Thompson's neighbor mentioning an auto accident?"

"Years ago. Skimmed over it."

"Right. I'll print out the transcript. Are you keen for a follow-up?" Maylee asked as the printer started to spit out paper.

****

"In a minute." Dave tossed the words toward the door as soon as his mind registered the sound of the knock. His hand stayed in motion and tossed another sock into the laundry basket. A glance out the peephole a moment later made him freeze. *Her.* He paused an instant to collect the good sense, which tended to flee when she came within sight.

He stepped into the hall, leaned against the door frame, and crossed his arms. "My, my, aren't you looking pleased with yourself. Did you come to arrest me?" He overemphasized his look toward the back door. "I don't see any back-up."

"I'm not here to take you into custody." Maylee widened her smile. "I do have news."

"Let me guess. You arrested a man and he confessed to Dr. Art's murder."

"Sorry. No. Good but not excellent type of information." She tipped her head and stared.

He glanced at her practical black shoes to bring another fleeing wit back home. As his gaze moved upward, over the long legs covered with khakis, past dark blue sweater and blazer, to a pearl earring peeking out between strands of pecan hair, he lost more control than a few breaths could recapture. The exterior package remained worthy of fantasy. Unfortunately, her occupation and handgun turned the image into a nightmare. "Speak."

"You…are cleared. Officially removed from the suspect list."

"The department approves of you spreading this information?" He adjusted his gaze as she performed a perfect swallow.

"My partner didn't object to my plan."

He nodded, expecting and dreading her to go upstairs and leave him alone with his housekeeping chores.

"Your hair. It's half gone."

"Your powers of observation are intact." He reached up and pushed spread fingers through the new style.

"I…I think I like it. It gives you a casual, yet controlled look. The shape reminds me of a surfer in a commercial."

"Thanks. Why did you really knock on my door?"

She skimmed her hands over her jacket pockets. "I'm going for a run. Want to join me?"

"When?" He knew he could change into running gear in less than three minutes. She'd have to take longer. She needed—he didn't even want to think the name—to transfer the dangerous metal thing on her hip in addition to changing clothes.

"Ten minutes."

"Got it." He pushed away from the wall and into the apartment in one continuous movement.

A moment later he leaned against the closed door and blew out a steady stream of tension. *Off the list. Confirmed my departure time.* The process of it didn't matter. They could have found a neighbor, spotted him on a camera, or interpreted body language of a dog for all he cared at this instant.

A minute later, as Dave tied his second sneaker, the first measure of Wagner's *Tannenhäuser* burst from his phone. *Sandra.* Typical of her to call when he didn't have time to spare. "Dave here."

"Are you driving? Can you talk?"

"I'm at home. Getting ready to go out." He carefully didn't mention details. Sandra didn't need encouragement to draw conclusions. If he mentioned going for a run with his neighbor, she would leap all the way to an imaginary engagement and wedding.

"Red, blue, or black?"

"Topic clue." He minimized his sigh. Sandra had a habit of starting in the middle of a subject.

"Flower pot. I'm standing in front of a beautiful display of prayer plants. Which color?"

He closed his eyes for an instant. With most people he'd suggest they decide. Sandra's mind didn't work like a majority of the population. "The one on the far right."

"Red it is, then. When should I bring it over?"

He picked up his baseball Cardinals cap and discovered it needed adjustment after his haircut. "Later. Two or three hours from now might be good."

"Honestly, David. Are you this rude with your

patients?"

No. You're special. He pressed his lips tight. "Really, I need to go. I'll see you later. After nine is best. I'll make it a point to be here then."

He ended the call, cased the phone, and left the apartment. If anyone, the mythical "they" for instance, attempted to chart his emotions and/or heart rate during the previous few days they better have paper ten times the capacity of the normal EKG strips. Since Friday afternoon he'd been running with a baseline of nervous caution with peaks of fearful panic. Apprehension, his nervous beast within, should be fit and lean with all his recent exercise. At least, Uncle Bob had talked him out of contacting a lawyer. Living in the same building as Maylee made her impossible to avoid entirely. After the elevator ride at the hospital, he'd half expected either her or her mint-loving partner to be behind every closed door, around every corner, or exiting any store he entered.

A few minutes pacing and stretching in the sunny parking lot, while waiting for Maylee, improved his mood tenfold. St. Louis was in bloom this week. He'd hold his breath when passing the lilacs during laps today.

****

Maylee set a fast walking pace for the three blocks from the apartment building to the entrance of Saxon Park. Weather and the recent losing streak of the Cardinals furnished conversation for the first portion. As they stepped from the feeder path to the wider jogging trail she lowered her narrow wrap-around sunglasses from hairband position.

They drew even with the lilacs marking the first

corner, and Dave increased the pace.

"Sprinting?" She listened for a response but only the sound of his light breathing and footsteps reached her.

He completed the turn and eased back to an endurance speed. "Experiment. Didn't work."

She flashed back to chemistry lab and a beaker of distillate that refused to turn the proper color as she added indicator from an eyedropper. It was good for the world, and her personal sanity, she studied a different branch of science.

"Brothers." She tossed the word to him a dozen paces later.

"I've one of those."

"Four. I learned to run keeping up with them."

"They taught you well."

She remained silent until they turned another corner. "Enough to catch the attention of the track coach. Did you run on a team?"

"Basketball. Running's for escape."

Interesting word choice. She released an easy laugh at the memory of Tom's parting comment today. He'd tapped the roof of his personal car to get her attention. Then, speaking in a voice loud enough for two patrol officers leaving the building to hear, advised her, "Go home and get to know your neighbor." At least, he exhibited enough sense to end it with a wink.

"Your dad a cop?" He expelled the words in a rush.

"Lawyer. Past tense. Dead three years. Heart attack." She eased the words out with a breathing technique combined from track and voice coaches. "Your dad a doctor?"

"No."

Ellen Parker

She waited a quarter of a lap for an explanation. They'd run a background on Dave while he was a suspect. Name, Sam Holmes, plus his birth and death dates, filled the information boxes for his father. She subtracted the death date, twenty-two years ago, from Dave's age and figured the loss of a parent when so young changed everything. When the report on Sandra arrived it explained a lot. The simple fact it arrived with a summary from the Department of Corrections made the listing of Robert Kale, an uncle, as emergency contact logical.

She planned to conceal the information she'd read on Sandra's rather lengthy report. It would be better to hear a voluntary explanation. "A barber?"

"Wrong again."

"Then what? He needed to make a living somehow." She glanced to her left but his profile remained unreadable.

"Machinist." He released the word as they paralleled the freeway in its artificial valley. "Chicken processing plant at the end. Marshall, Missouri. I'm thinking you read this information on a report."

"Background requested was yours. Not his." *Your mother's came later.*

They settled into an easy silence for several laps. The only place they exchanged more than a few words at a time occurred on the Grand Avenue leg of the route. Pedestrian traffic increased, and they slowed the pace enough to trade brief comments about the statues of notable German immigrants in the plaza.

As they passed the small clump of weeping willows, she held up one finger for the number of laps remaining. She lagged half a pace to get a clear look toward the dog park. One of her favorite cool down routines included a lap or two on the grass around the fenced area. Often she would linger to watch the dogs and chat with an owner or two.

"What?" Dave pointed off to their right. "No."

A woman, a small boy, and one large dog stood between the double dog run gates, either coming or going. As she watched between blinks, the situation changed.

Without a word to each other, she and Dave sprinted toward the tall, sturdy fence surrounding the pet area.

The large black dog broke into a run. A dark-haired boy stayed on the far end of the leash, trying to keep up on short legs. The woman hobbled after them, falling behind, and calling, "*Rufus. Colin.*"

Maylee sensed Dave on her left, keeping pace and staring at the leashed pair pulling away from the adult. When they had closed to within a dozen yards of the dog, she eased her pace, raised two fingers to her mouth, and whistled.

Dave surged forward, scooped up the boy, and pushed him against the side of a van.

A box truck emblazoned with a moving company logo rumbled past.

The dog paused on the far side of the street and gazed back toward Maylee.

"Nice dog. Good Rufus." She checked for traffic and crossed the street with quick strides. Keeping eye contact with Rufus, she continued to talk to the dog in an even voice until she picked up the nylon leash. "Come. Heel."

"He's not hurt, ma'am." Dave lifted the boy away

from the van and carried him over to where his mother sat awkwardly on the grass. "What happened?"

"It's my fault." The woman hugged her son close. "Next time, if it happens again"—she wiped tears with the back of one hand—"drop the leash."

"May I?" Dave pointed to the tall fracture boot encasing the woman's left foot. He squatted down, asked about her injury, and checked the multiple Velcro straps.

"Sit." Maylee commanded Rufus when they arrived within a few steps of the mother and child. She listened as Dave posed questions and the woman replied in a shaky voice. *Injured foot.* It explained the parent's lack of speed. It may even explain why such a large, strong dog was mismatched with a young boy.

"Thank you. From the bottom of my heart, I never…" The mother began to push up, and Dave wrapped one of her hands around his forearm.

"Are you safe to drive?" Dave asked.

"I will be. I'm sorry. And grateful."

"No problem, ma'am." Maylee tugged Rufus back into a sit as he attempted to reach his people. "Rufus is well trained. Have you owned him long?"

"My dog." Colin spoke for the first time. "Uncle Ed gave him to me."

Maylee looked at the mother for more explanation.

"He moved. Uncle Ed. We figured Rufus would do better here than in an apartment in Little Rock. He suggested an obedience class. Guess we better sign up." She reached for the leash, but Maylee shook her head.

"I'll get him into your vehicle. And yes, class is a good idea." She gave silent thanks and smiled.

A few minutes later, Maylee and Dave walked

away toward home. The family sat secure in their van. Dave had extracted a promise from the woman not to drive for another five minutes while she gathered the remainder of her nerves.

"Impressive." Dave shook his wrists as if releasing tension.

"Not bad yourself."

"I meant the whistle. Did your brothers teach you?"

She adjusted the sunglasses perched in her hair and smiled. "Dad. He taught all of us."

"Hunting dogs?"

"Hardly. We fostered service dogs. The agency we worked with figured if a puppy could survive from weaning to eighteen months or so in our household they could behave in public."

"And did they?"

She resisted the urge to grasp his hand and walk along the street like good friends. "After the children and puppy both learned the curriculum, the dogs went on to serve honorably."

"And the children?"

"We took longer."

Chapter Eight

Maylee selected a leaf rake with bright orange plastic tines from the hand tool display. She rubbed her palm against the handle to test the finish and tuned into the conversations drifting around her. Leaf & Turf Landscaping hummed with families carrying plastic containers and pushing carts of plants in rich, peaty dirt. She'd not expected Tuesday early evening to be such a popular time at a garden center.

"From the grandsons." She handed the rake to Steve, her oldest brother. "How are you and your allergies coping around all this vegetation?"

"Good." He strummed the tines as if harp strings. "I take my meds and substitute cola for beer like an obedient patient."

"Glad to hear you stay safe to drive. I'd hate to arrest my own brother for stupidity."

"Last I heard, lack of common sense didn't constitute a crime." He twirled the rake and turned the conversation. "I can see the little rascals presenting this with great ceremony. I think Michelle can find something in her collection of gift bows to make it memorable."

"No doubt." Maylee turned her gaze to Kate, who stood across the counter, scanning the claim ticket for the black gum shade tree and the containers of annuals. The tree, selected from half a dozen candidates, was destined for Dianne Morgan's front yard. The petunias and pansies would find a new home in Michelle's flower bed.

Her friend wore a cheerful face, subdued only to acquaintances able to compare it to her usual, more genuine smile. *You don't need to know. Not yet.* Thursday, two days in the future, when she walked into the visitation for Kate's uncle, Art Saterro, her friend would know Maylee worked the case. She hoped they could share good news by then. She, Tom, and several others had completed dozens of interviews and followed tips. Stalled—every last one of them reached a dead end of one sort or another.

"We'll be open until nine this Saturday." Kate handed Steve a bright yellow claim ticket. "Which brother did you say would be stopping in?"

"Matthew. He's got the best truck for the job."

Was that her "I've got a secret" grin? Maylee focused her gaze on Kate's face, checking for the sparkle usually accompanying the already vanished super smile.

"Be sure he brings the pick-up stub. It's a real hassle to sort it out otherwise."

"Steve, you better keep it at your place." Maylee grasped the rake.

He gathered up the box of bedding plants. "I intended to. I'm familiar with the odds of finding you at home."

"So am I." She reached over the counter and tapped Kate's hand for attention. "Take care of yourself. We'll make a date and have a long talk over pizza. Soon."

"In the interim, get in a run for me. And prayers for

Mom. She's taking Uncle Art's death hard." Kate sighed. "Luci and Maria have moved in with her until your department releases the house. Any idea when they'll be able to return home?"

Maylee pressed her lips tight. The crime lab controlled the scene, in consultation with her captain. "You'll get word any day now."

"Yesterday would have been good."

"Be careful what you wish for." *Tony isn't cleared yet.* Maylee skimmed down the mental list of neighbors and employees of Mr. Tony Lorenti. None of them had seen or spoken to the man during the critical hours of late Wednesday and early Thursday. It remained premature to remove him from the suspect list. She avoided the need for further comment as the next customer stepped up to the counter.

"Do you want to come over? Should I call in the two minute warning?" Steve positioned the rake across the back seat of his older, compact car a few moments later.

"Not tonight. I'm planning on going home and getting a run in before dark." Maylee waved to her brother and walked toward her Camry in the next row. A run would be good to drain away some of the job stress. Maybe she'd invite Dave. She smiled at the memory of yesterday's walk home after the incident at the dog park. Conversation of dogs, basketball, and bad movies seen during high school made the time pleasant.

Twenty minutes later, Maylee pulled mail out of the narrow box and pushed the brass lid back into place. She tucked the handful of envelopes and flyers into a pocket and headed for Dave's door.

"One minute."

Inviting scents, including onions, peppers, and apples escaped from his apartment. The sweet and spicy air shifted her palate into "feed me" mode. Easing back a step she smiled in line with the peephole.

"Arrest him yet?" He spoke as he leaned forward, filling the partial width of the open door with his bare shoulders.

Maylee swallowed once…twice. *Skin. Muscles. Pale hair.* For an instant she feared drowning. "Arrest? Not yet. Still working on it. Uh…would you like to run at Saxon Park?"

"Not tonight. I've company coming over."

"Of course." Her mouth went from flood to drought. "Another time? Tomorrow?" She adjusted her stance when he smiled. Neighbors shouldn't look this good without shirts. They should have obvious flaws instead of taut skin decorated with blond curls. She rubbed her fingers against each other to keep them from reaching out to caress his chest.

"I'll keep it in mind." He hesitated before settling his lips into a shape worthy of a lip balm commercial.

"Good." She swallowed again and focused on his generous smile. The words on her tongue swapped places in line, gawked at inviting lips before forming into sensible order when she closed her mouth for an instant. "I'll leave you to your plans. Smells like your guest will be getting a great meal."

He laughed. "Talk to you tomorrow."

She fled up the steps and all the way to her door without drawing another breath.

"Stupid me. Making assumptions and paying in embarrassment." She rambled to her empty apartment. Her body carried out the routine tasks of getting a drink of water and removing Angel, her weapon. She set the Glock 19 on the table and coiled her wide belt beside it. The mail crinkled in her pocket as she removed her jacket. At the audio prompt, she sorted through the envelopes. Phone bill and the monthly coupon offers landed beside her handgun, and she stared at the remaining piece.

Trick advertising? She turned over the business-size envelope and inspected it for a company or personal name. Nothing. The handwritten block letters of her name and address didn't look familiar. The stamp was one of the recent "forever" designs available everywhere. She found a knife and slit the envelope. A single typed sheet fell on the kitchen counter.

Pinpricks of caution visited the nape of her neck, and she steadied her breath while using the knife to smooth the paper open.

Justice delayed a man can accept. The letter was printed in a common font, black ink on white paper, exactly like a majority of the computer printers in use. *Can't abide justice denied. Crime ignored.*

The sins of the father. You drew the honor.

Confused? Research the day before the world changed. Follow the tragedy's trail of errors to your doorstep. Discover the black heart beating in Gary Morgan's chest. No surprise it sputtered to an end.

"My father?" She stared at his name, searched for a reason it should appear now, three years past his death.

Payment is past due.

I'll stay in touch.

She stared at the words, let them drift out of focus and back again. She counted three deep breaths before checking the clock. "Of all the…."

Using a plastic bag, kitchen tongs, and a felt tip marker, Maylee improvised an evidence bag for the letter and envelope. Then she dialed Tom while returning her Glock to her hip and shrugging into her jacket. *Pick up. Don't be away from your phone.* She listened to it click into voice mail. "This is Morgan. I've got a situation. Can you meet me at the lab?"

****

Dave tightened his grip on the edge of the door until his tendons ached. His gaze remained on the sliver of stairway long after Maylee's feet moved out of sight. He listened to her soft footsteps overhead and exhaled when her door closed.

Too close. He shut his door and leaned against it, willing his common sense to return from the corners of the universe where it'd fled the instant he spied her through the peephole.

He closed his eyes for a moment and recalled her image. A pale, high neck sweater under a dark jacket revealed nothing aside from feminine curves. One lock of pecan hair begged him to reach out and hook it behind her ear, to give a full view of the small pearl earring. His mind strayed to her mouth, the hesitation in the lips kissed with pale pink gloss. His lips twitched as if asking if her mouth would be flavored sweet as cotton candy or tinted with mint. He suspected from hesitation in her voice she'd struggled a little to extend the invitation.

Good. We may as well both be caught off balance. A few moments ago, when she'd stood outside his door commenting on the stew aroma, he'd teetered on the edge of foolishness. Only her hasty exit prevented him from breaking his top house rule and inviting a woman with a gun to step inside to share supper.

He pushed away from the door and forced his attention on the biscuit ingredients waiting next to the cup of milk. He poured, mixed, and talked to the quiet kitchen. "Company. Of all the words to use. No, it's a safe description. Let her think it's female. Young. Competition."

With quick sure circles of his hand on the wide wood board he prepared the surface to roll the biscuits. He turned his thoughts to Uncle Bob. Conversation with a rational man was exactly what he needed tonight. Every word between staff at the clinic this week perched on the edge between polite and strained. Only the patients hinted at a normal world where it wasn't against the rules to use the full range of emotion.

When the biscuits lay on the pan waiting for the oven, he washed his hands and then pulled on the clean T-shirt waiting on the back of a chair. He heard the building door and glanced out the dining area window.

"Where is she going? Those aren't her jogging clothes?" He glanced at the floor, self-conscious of talking to an empty room.

Half an hour later, Dave rose from the table to adjust the blinds clicking in a sudden gust of wind. He checked the parking lot for the umpteenth time. Maylee's parking space remained empty. He shouldn't care.

"Good supper. It's a shame Joan is working tonight." Uncle Bob pushed his empty bowl away.

"I'll send a container home with you. Aunt Joan can impress her co-workers during her supper break tomorrow."

"You better send the recipe, too. I'm guessing this

one's a keeper."

"Yeah, sure thing." Dave gathered up dirty dishes while hunting for the next conversation topic. Over a Highlands stew he'd adapted from the mission kitchen, they'd discussed weather, baseball, and toasted his official removal from the police suspect list.

"Did you talk to Sandra today?" Bob swirled the lone, small, ice cube in his glass.

"Briefly. I offered to take her to the Botanical Gardens on Sunday. She hasn't picked a place to eat. Guess I shouldn't be surprised if she waits until the last minute." He sighed at the recitation of their incomplete Mother's Day plans. Since her release from prison, Sandra insisted on spending huge portions of the holiday with one or both of her sons. Dave frequently cut his time with her short due to call and study hours during his student and training days. He was out of excuses this year.

"She'll like the attention."

"Have you met her friend Larry?"

Bob carried the last dishes to the sink. "No. She's talked about him. I gave up trying to understand her and her taste in men years ago. Why do you ask?"

Dave shrugged. "I've seen him twice now. First time, we met downtown for supper before one of their Thursday AA meetings. Then Sunday, they stopped over to see the apartment."

"First impression?"

"Quiet. Seems to care for Sandra. My intuition tells me he's not as sober as he lets on." He scooped the last of the stew into a plastic container. "Weird thing happened as they left Sunday."

"I'm listening."

Dave straightened, sorted through some of his own unpleasant surprise at the brief encounter with Maylee. He may be off the suspect list, but even the mental name of her occupation brought sweat to the back of his neck. Sunday afternoon, while still on the suspect list, he'd held an internal wrestling match to stay in control. "As I walked Sandra and Larry out on Sunday, the detective from upstairs came home. Yes, I managed introductions. It was Larry's reaction that startled me. He paled as much as I did when Aaron's friend brought a rifle over to the house years ago. I'd guess he was ten seconds from passing out. Has Sandra told you his history? Is he apt to be wanted for something?"

"Not anything she mentioned. I don't think Sandra collects a detailed background on her male companions. They might ask her the wrong questions in return."

Dave nodded. He could imagine Sandra evading an answer to "where were you when…" Did she give only the small Missouri town for an answer? Her list of people needing the details of her life was short. Like his own. "You're right there. She manages to keep to the recent past very well."

"So do you." Bob stared until Dave felt heat and color in his cheeks.

"I'm working on it." He'd perfected evasive answers to classmates when they asked about his mother. A simple "she's away" worked for the first year or two. Later, as he and his friends got a little more sophisticated, he implied she stayed in rehab out of town. It was close to the truth. If you considered state prison a rehab facility. At least, she stayed off alcohol during her stay. Although even sober, she didn't get any better at answering Dave's primary question during visits. *Why? Why not a divorce?*

"I read in the paper Dr. Saterro's funeral will be Friday. Are you going?"

Dave rubbed at an invisible spot on the worn table. "I'll pay my respects at the visitation. They decided to keep the clinic open, and I volunteered." He fisted his hand around the disposable wipe. "They'll have a full church. It's not like my absence will be noticed."

Bob studied him with a parental gaze, a look that had the ability to make him feel ten years old and needing to explain a damaged bicycle. "I'll cope. An arrest will help. If you have information, feel free to share with my neighbor."

"I'm guessing you don't mean the elderly woman who waylaid me in the hall." Bob turned away and looked at the books on the top shelf. "She said good things about you. Positive comments a paragraph long on the food smells coming out of your place. She likes your new haircut. I did detect a bit of matchmaker gleam when she mentioned how nice to have more than one young person in the building."

"Mrs. Gossen will be in the book under nosy neighbor." *Maylee is filed under pretty and deadly.*

Chapter Nine

Warm air, carrying the heavy, sweet scent of too many flowers, punched Dave in the stomach the moment he stepped into South City Funeral Home. His beast called "Apprehension" awoke and began exercising. *Ignore the lilacs.* He steadied his breathing and walked past an arrangement of tulips, lilacs, and lilies on a tall stand. This was necessary. The family, the survivors, deserved to know they, and Dr. Saterro, mattered. Dave nodded to a stranger in a black suit and paused to enter his name in the guest book. If he controlled his emotions for the next hour or so he would be done. By volunteering to work at the clinic tomorrow, he would avoid the funeral and graveside services.

Too much black. He forced a neutral expression when he spotted Maylee's partner in a knot of men under an ornate light fixture. He scanned the room and located his neighbor in conversation with an elderly woman. *Too many detectives.*

"Holmes." He flinched as a hand rested on his shoulder before the voice registered as a friendly acquaintance.

"Garrison. Anything new since this morning?" He managed a steady voice, much like the one he and this final year resident shared in the operating suite earlier in the day.

"Nothing to write home about. I'm going to miss the man. Have you spoken to the family yet?"

"I arrived all of thirty seconds ago. You?" He glanced toward the receiving line of widow, daughter, and a large man with an authoritative air.

"Obligation complete."

Dave tucked a smile behind serious, straight lips. Garrison showed the talent and personality to do well in the world. In a few short weeks, the current surgical resident and his wife would move away to join a practice in Laramie, Wyoming. "I'll take my turn. Perhaps we can socialize after."

Ten minutes later, his condolences expressed to the family, Dave joined Garrison and one of the surgical nurses. Medical matters and Cardinal baseball flowed in the conversation.

"Got a minute?" Dave shrank from the voice and a whiff of mint.

He backed away from the others and faced Maylee's partner. *Wilson, his name is Wilson.* Couldn't he have this time, already mentally difficult, sans personal detective interview? "I've told you everything. More than twice."

"This isn't about you."

Dave exhaled. "Then who?"

"How long have you known Lawrence Thompson?"

Dave stiffened. What did the police want with Sandra's friend? Did Larry's reaction to Maylee on Sunday actually have a meaning? The creature in his stomach performed back flips. "Not long. Do you need the precise day?"

"I'm looking for your first impression."

"He managed a normal conversation." *Unlike me, at the moment.*

"Give it another try. Would you believe a story he told?"

"Sandra's taste in men...it's...I seldom have anything in common with them." He studied the detective's face and didn't learn anything valuable. A simple background check, which the police would run long before asking him questions about Larry, would give them more information than he gathered from two casual meetings.

"Sandra." Detective Wilson reached into his pocket. "Your mother?"

Dave nodded. "She's widowed." He swallowed down the summary of how it happened and let the moisture distract Apprehension. "She seldom lacks male companionship for long. Larry's been around...I'm not sure, several months."

"Good to know." He offered a mint.

Dave fumbled with the wrapper for a moment.

"Detective Morgan's good at what she does. She refuses to date cops."

"You tell me this because?"

"General information. Useful trivia." He popped a mint into his mouth. "If you run well enough, you might be able to catch her."

Dave gave the older man a puzzled look. *Literally or figuratively?* "She's a difficult person to ignore. Considering where we live."

"Yes, she told me the neighbor bit. Take care, doc." He ambled away to a group including a priest.

Dave sighed and studied Maylee talking with a middle-aged couple. She turned, sighted him, and smiled. Living downstairs from a gun-toting beauty kept his nerves on edge.

****

"If you're serious about putting in a rock garden, I suggest you talk to your neighbor's niece." Maylee turned to point out Kate to Betty Fielding. "She's over there, with the black and silver shawl."

"This is hardly the time or place."

"I'm sure she'll be glad to talk plants. At the very least, you can get the proper name of her employer. It's one of the larger places out by Earth City. I can find it but not remember the exact title. Does the same thing happen to you?" She held her lips small and level while reciting the complete name and address of the landscape company in silence. Lies, even small ones to get reluctant bystanders to talk, went against her nature.

"All the time." Betty emphasized her words with a nod. "I'm poor at giving directions, too. I mention places out of business or sometimes even torn down. Guess it comes with living my entire life in one city."

"And then God invented the GPS." Maylee packed the phrase in a smile.

"Those aren't foolproof, or Betty-proof, either. We haven't owned one yet able to decipher the one-way streets in my home neighborhood."

"Dutchtown? Am I right you grew up there?" Maylee pictured those streets, specifically the one where her brother lived in their childhood home. Until a few years ago they allowed two-way traffic plus parking in both directions. Getting them re-designated saved many fenders and much frustration when meeting a garbage or delivery truck. She resisted mentioning Thompson until his sister opened the topic.

109

"Three blocks from church and school. Most of the homes have changed hands a couple of times. Except for Mr. Mueller"—she dropped her voice—"and Larry."

Maylee replayed a portion of the second interview with Mr. Mueller. The elderly man took the circuitous route in conversation, but managed to remark Larry's truck moved from the driveway to the street between sunset and sunrise on the date Dr. Saterro was murdered.

"Is my wife insulting herself in public?" John Fielding joined the ladies.

"I was commenting on my sense of direction. Or rather, the lack thereof." Betty touched his arm in a spousal signal.

"She inherited it from her father. Larry, on the other hand..." John looked at Maylee directly. "He could find his way home drunk without headlights. Probably has."

"Recently?" According to his warehouse co-workers, Larry had been sober for the three years they worked together. His army buddy and Larry's own words contradicted the statement. They both admitted to talking and drinking their way through a twelve-pack eight nights ago. It could prove important if he strayed in the last few weeks and bluffed his way past his co-workers.

"Not certain. He's gotten better at hiding it. If he wants to live much longer, he'll not mix it with his prescription meds. How many does he take?" He addressed his wife.

Betty shrugged. "Five, six, it seems to change all the time. Last year I accused him of doctor shopping.

He didn't take it well."

"Few people would." Maylee knew the advertisements constantly reminded people to check with their physicians and discuss medications before adding anything new. It was logical. Unfortunately, she interacted daily with a population oblivious to common sense. She moved her gaze around the room and paused on Dave listening to another physician from the clinic.

"Do you know him?" Betty interrupted her next patterned scan of the room.

"Who?"

"Gray suit. Red and silver tie. I dare say I wouldn't mind an introduction."

John cleared his throat. "Don't mind my wife. Her secret ambition is matchmaker."

"I've met the man in question." Maylee gave silent thanks her modest blouse minimized others noticing the blush heating her neck. Her pulse had jumped ten minutes ago when he arrived and each time her gaze skimmed the room and located him it stuttered. As planned, Tom drew him into conversation for several moments. Now he glanced her way before turning back to a cluster of clinic employees. "Any luck matching up your brother?"

Betty chewed her lower lip for a moment as if reluctant to respond. "He does fine on his own. He bought a diamond once. Barbara…can't remember her last name. She died. Traffic accident. Larry took it hard."

Maylee nodded silent encouragement to continue.

"Larry was going to get refused," John mumbled.

"You know this because…?" Betty opened her eyes wider.

"We talked. Barbara expressed serious concern about his intentions a few days before she died." Jim looked at his wife. "At the Labor Day picnic your mother hosted, the last of them held at her house. Since then they've been at our place. Remember?"

"What sort of concerns?" Maylee forced casual into her question.

"Barbara told me she liked Larry but not his drinking. I got the feeling he needed to make a choice between the beer or the girl."

"How many years ago did this happen?"

John shrugged. "Ten? Twelve? Can't remember for certain."

Maylee tucked the information next to the memory of the records they'd been reviewing since the threatening letter appeared at her apartment. More than a decade was a long time to let hatred simmer. Not impossible, she decided at the memory of Larry's eyes during Dave's hasty introductions on Sunday.

"Excuse us." John cupped his wife's elbow.

"Of course." Maylee nodded as they eased away toward the exit. She scanned the room from closed casket to the receiving line.

Luci shook her head as Tony talked. A moment later the widow jabbed one finger at her brother's chest and mouthed several words. It reminded Maylee of her mother confronting Matt coming home at sunrise.

In the next moment, Kate swept in from the direction of the guest book and guided her Uncle Tony toward the foyer.

Maylee hurried across the room, making sure to bump Detective Johnson's elbow as she passed, and paused at the coatrack. From down the hall, where a door stood open to a small, empty office, she picked out Kate's angry tone.

"This is not the time or place."

Maylee pictured her friend pacing, the ends of her shawl waving with each word she spoke.

"Not your decision." Tony's low voice rumbled.

Maylee pointed Johnson, selected because he'd never interviewed Tony, toward the tiny room. He sauntered down the hall, checking doors and looking very much like a confused guest hunting for the restroom.

"Charity dear to her heart." Tony punctuated his speech with a snort. "Get real, Kate. Children of the Far Hills is blood money—a guilt donation. It's time for it to stop."

Kate's reply vanished as a door clicked closed.

Maylee tapped the charity name into her smartphone as she walked out the front door. Tony may have turned the lagging financial portion of the investigation in a new direction.

Chapter Ten

Dave leaned against his Prius and examined the western sky. All the darker shades of gray were displayed in lobulated clouds. Ignoring the color and concentrating on the shapes alone, it could be a textbook photo of fatty tissue. He tipped his head and closed his eyes to savor the first gust of cool air.

Until a few minutes ago, the day had been sunny and hot, only a degree off the record at the airport. "Midwest May weather," he mouthed to the sky, "everything except boring."

"Are you coming inside?"

He snapped his eyes open and turned to face Mrs. Gossen standing on the back step. "Soon. Do you need something?"

"I don't know about your generation, doc. Mine. We have enough sense to come in out of the rain. Laundry room," she continued without pause, "when the sirens go off I expect to see you. Safest place in the building."

He lifted a hand to acknowledge her. His next-door neighbor loved the sound of her own voice. Or perhaps she feared silence. Either way he understood during their first meeting it was best to treat her as social media. Don't say a word you don't want the entire world to know by sundown.

"You can do me a favor by taking this out to the

dumpster." She pointed to the half full trash bag at her feet. "Yes, I know the truck won't be by until Monday. I'm also aware the tuna tin will be stinking up half the apartments by then. You like tuna? What did you cook the other night? It smelled good. Almost a light barbeque. I took the liberty to introduce myself to your guest. Your uncle? Nice man. It's easy to see where you get your good looks."

Dave set his backpack next to his car and took the few steps to her garbage sack. Should he even try to slide an answer into her monologue? "That would have been the spicy beef stew in the slow cooker."

"Crock pot sort of cook. Figures. My daughter uses hers a lot. Works out good, she's got one of those jobs which require overtime almost regular. I'd like to see her be home a little more. But the money's good. She took the grandkids to Florida on their spring break. She gets to travel more than I ever did. Change of times. Oh, I'm glad for her, don't get me wrong."

"Pardon me." He picked up the bag and crossed the parking lot to the dumpster. A single panel of privacy fence shielded the large bin on a concrete pad from the street. When he turned around, Mrs. Gossen had gone inside.

He shrugged, picked up his pack, and looked at the sky for another long moment. The clouds rolled toward the east, pulling their unique excitement over the city. He let his mind drift back to another storm, the year he was nine.

"Last one to the park feeds the dog." He and his Cousin Aaron raced toward the neighborhood playground on their bikes. They arrived and dropped their rides beside the parking strip as three women

herded smaller children into cars.

"Swings."

"Slide." Dave challenged a few rumbles of thunder later. He dashed up the ladder and lifted his arms high. It was a bad scene from a cheap movie. But the rush, the thrill as the wind lifted his hair almost straight up filled him with joy.

"Stupid." Aaron called from below. "That's electricity up there. Headed this way."

Dave delayed for another moment before sliding down.

They hurried to their bikes and raced away. Before they reached the park entrance, lightning darted down. He felt the air get sucked out of his chest and then replaced with the sizzle and scent of scorched wood. A tree at the edge of the play area released a thread of smoke.

A shiver danced across his shoulders at the vivid memory. "Too close even for me. I don't think we ever told Uncle Bob about the incident."

A few minutes after Dave entered his apartment the tornado warning sirens started. He pushed his feet into old running shoes and glanced out the window. The air had darkened to a deep dusk with a hint of malicious green added to gray. Every tree within sight waved branches in an improvised flexibility competition.

He tucked keys into his pocket, grabbed a flashlight and extra batteries from a drawer, and headed for the basement laundry room.

"It's about time." Mrs. Gossen sat in the lone fiberglass chair clutching her rosary. "Building's almost empty. Pray all the others are in safe places. Do you know Glen?"

A stooped man turned from tuning a small radio on the table. He skimmed a hand across his bald head before extending it to Dave. "Glen Moss. International Brotherhood of Electrical Workers. Retired."

"Dave Holmes. At the other end of my career."

"It's a pleasure."

Thunder and the lash of rain against the single high window replaced the sound of the mechanical siren. The fluorescent tube ceiling fixtures began to flicker, magnifying the effect of lightning outside.

Glen muttered over the radio and moved it around until the announcer's voice outweighed the static.

Dave leaned against a washer and turned his mind to the minutia of the day. He and three others comprised the entire office staff today. The only patients arriving at the clinic consisted of those driving in from a distance and a handful who could not wait until Monday. For the entire day, voices remained soft, the tone subdued.

Mrs. Gossen clutched her black beads and recited the history of past storms and their damage.

Crash. Rumble. Rumble.

"They're getting closer." Glen bumped the table and his flashlight dropped.

"This looks like a cozy group." Maylee stood in the doorway.

"How is it outside? Lights have flickered already, radio's talking about Jefferson County." Mrs. Gossen raised the silver crucifix to her lips.

Maylee pushed both hands through her hair, releasing a cascade of fine droplets. "Wild. Signals are out at Jefferson and Russell."

"And you didn't stay to direct traffic?" Glen asked.

"Patrol was already on site." She took two steps forward and squatted down to pick up the rolling flashlight.

Crash. Rumble. The lights shook and went out.

Dave straightened and opened his arms. Suddenly they filled with Maylee. Her wet wool suit and soft curves molded to his embrace. He held her closer than necessary and detected the scent of tropical flowers. "You okay?"

"Now I am." She stiffened in a silent request to be released.

He hesitated. She felt right in his arms. He adjusted his fingers on her shoulders and leaned forward. His cheek brushed her ear and the texture begged for exploration. He touched his lips against her skin in a soft kiss. He held his breath, reluctant to disturb the magic connection. For an instant, an eternity, he feathered kisses down her neck.

"May…" The hip holster under her suit jacket pressed against his body, turning it to ice. "Later." He lingered his lips a millimeter away from her neck as the heat from their recent contact counterbalanced the freezing low in his body. "We need to talk."

She eased back and shielded her eyes as Mrs. Gossen switched on a heavy-duty light aimed at her face. "Affirmative."

Glen snatched the light away and pointed it to the ceiling. "Careful with your spotlight. You could blind a person."

Maylee breathed a sigh and leaned against the washer beside Dave. "Remind me not to be standing on one foot the next time the lights go out."

"Check. I'll put it on the list of dangerous tasks.

Would you suggest one or two slots below making an opening incision during an earthquake?" He held his breath as she failed to conceal a giggle. For a moment he thought she would speak.

"Heels." Mrs. Gossen broke her thirty-second silence. "Since when do you wear fancy shoes? All I've ever seen in the years you've been here is sensible shoes, like rubber-soled oxfords. Unless you're off duty. The rest of you…did you work in a skirt? What's going on?"

Dave hid his smile behind his hand on the chance the older woman could see more than expected in the subdued lighting.

"I attended a funeral. Dressed for the occasion, nothing more to say about it."

Dave clicked on his flashlight and laid it in the seam between the two washers. "I expect you had a good crowd."

She brushed remaining raindrops off the tight weave of her suit coat sleeves and looked at him. "Guests overflowed into the fellowship hall. I didn't see you."

"I worked. I don't care much for funerals."

"Not all of them can be avoided."

"True." He flinched at another close lightning strike.

"My word, this is a long storm." Mrs. Gossen lapsed back into her recitation of her personal experiences in violent weather interspersed with phrases from rosary prayers.

Dave stared at his toes and drifted into the past. The first and worst funeral he attended in his life returned with talking shadows.

"Come on, Joe." Dave grasped his brother's hand and stood up. He concentrated on the next portion as Aunt Joan and Uncle Bob had explained it. If he thought of it as the next step in a full-page math problem he could do it. First you add. That was entering the church and conquering the urge to sneeze among all the flowers.

Then you subtract. He'd counted and recounted the stars in the painted arch behind the altar while the pastor droned.

Multiply. Sit still while strangers took turns saying meaningless things to the friends, relatives, and curious neighbors gathered in the small room.

Write the answer. He drew a little courage from the sharp scent of freshly extinguished candles. He stepped into the aisle and held tight to Joe's hand as they followed their father out into the hot August sunshine.

A warm touch on his hand jerked him into the present.

"Earth to Dave," Maylee prompted. "Have a nice trip?"

"Not particularly." He disliked those journeys into the past. Sometimes, like today, with the spoken and implied questions of funerals, he understood what prompted them. Other times one of the multiple doors to the past would swing open without warning and overpower logic. But he always returned a little embarrassed when others guessed he'd gone on a mental vacation. "Is the worst of the storm over?"

"According to the radio," Glen replied.

He pushed away from Maylee's touch and picked up his flashlight. He needed a moment to lock the door on the memory. Plus, Maylee with the beautiful legs, intelligence, and a sense of humor radiated magnetic waves toward him. He pressed his lips and remembered the clean taste of spring rain on her skin. She personified everything he'd ever imagined in a girlfriend—except for the addition of a gun at her hip.

"What do you think?" Dave directed his words to Glen, the safest target. "Three, four minutes and then we go check for damage?"

****

Second by creeping second, the radio announcer's voice won the airwaves from the static. Maylee sighed out a measure of relief at the announcement when the National Weather Service changed the tornado warning on the Missouri side of the river to the far less threatening thunderstorm watch.

She studied Dave without changing her casual stance. Better lighting would have been good a few minutes ago, when he drifted out of the present. The word "firearms" triggered a similar reaction during the interview. What did we say or do today?

Mrs. Gossen cleared her throat and pronounced, "Amen."

"Shall we go?" Maylee pushed away from the washer and fought the urge to reach up and touch where warm kisses so recently danced across her skin. Practical matters delayed a conversation with Dave.

"Allow me." Glen hurried to the door. "I'll go out the front entrance and check the east side of the property."

"We'll take the back." Dave turned and touched her elbow.

Maylee flinched at a mini-bolt of personal

lightning and took a calming breath.

Mrs. Gossen stood and turned off the radio. "Men. Haven't met one yet who knows how to turn off an electrical gadget. Need to save the batteries until they get us back up and running. One time it took four days."

"That specific power outage happened years ago. They do much better now. Not more than an hour or two at a time since I moved in." Maylee added her penlight to the rays of illumination.

"When did your move happen?" Dave followed two paces behind.

"Two years last February. I don't recommend winter moves. But I had a situation." She suppressed a shudder. Combine an old heating system, broken pipe, and overtime at work to delay discovery and the apartment became unlivable. So she rescued what she could during a hectic night of packing. Her brothers helped with vehicles and manpower, but it still meant a lot of cold hours, confusion, and frantic search for a new apartment within the city. She forced a quick pace up the steps.

"We may have another." Dave's voice came from close to her shoulder.

She glimpsed the door to the parking lot and stopped so sudden he brushed up against her back. A quick swallow tempered the heat seeping through her best black suit coat. The large glass panel of the parking lot door hung shattered in place. It appeared as if one touch and it would crumble into thousands of bits of safety glass. She pushed against the wide metal frame prepared to jump out of the way. "I don't think we want to slam this."

"Thank you, Miss Obvious." He added his hand to the frame as she stepped through.

"*Holy Mother of God!*" She didn't attempt to stop both hands from rising to her cheeks as she stopped two steps into the asphalt parking lot.

"I'll second that."

Maylee found enough good sense to walk around the back of Dave's car and paused behind her Camry. A Bradford pear, upright on the boulevard strip when she parked less than a quarter hour ago, lay sprawled across the hood of her car. The entire tree, all thirty odd feet of it, spread out on display. The root ball dripped mud at the point of origin while the trunk blocked the sidewalk and the largest branches rested against dented silver sheet metal. Scars in the bark indicated places where the branches contacted and bounced off the sedan's windshield support posts before halting above the headlights. Smaller branches and a mass of leaves hid the front of the orange Prius. "My brother Matt is right. I need to put my insurance agent on speed dial."

She sighed, pulled out her phone, and began taking damage photos. She squatted for the best angle and ignored the light rain feeding the shallow parking lot puddles. The dangerous part of the storm was over; these remnants would do nothing more than make clean up wet and inconvenient. She glanced down to check her footing and warmed under Dave's gaze. "What's so interesting?"

"Oh…nothing." He kicked a small piece of debris.

"Well, pardon me. This wasn't my first choice of activity this afternoon either." She marched past him and circumvented the tangled, muddy roots.

"Not your first insurance claim?" He retreated to a

spot between the cars.

She eased into the narrow space between leafy branches and the building. "It's the first involving a tree. And earlier this week I thought I'd convinced my partner to let me drive. Good-bye to driving on duty this month. Unless I snatch the keys as he collapses laughing."

"You weren't driving when this happened."

"It's never mattered before." She braced her back against the building and photographed headlight and grill damage. The four incidents paraded past in her memory.

"The first was the worst." She didn't continue with the description of crouching behind her assigned cruiser while it absorbed half a dozen bullets before being rammed.

She'd actually been inside the car during the second accident. Her hand held the keys about six inches from the ignition at the moment the drunk clipped her faithful, faded Corolla. She banished the memory only to have the incident from four months ago replace it. Second week as a detective, first day Tom allowed her behind the wheel. The slam of their doors still echoed along the street when the distraught homeowner crashed into the sedan's trunk.

And now…She shook her head at the speed this would spread. The men in the homicide division, with their motorized egos, would take their teasing up to, but not over, the edge of harassment. It came with the job. She gave silent thanks for four brothers who toughened her skin before she entered the academy.

"It looks like I'll be able to back mine out of the forest." Dave reached into the flexible small branches with tiny, new leaves resting on the Prius bumper and hood. "I know where we can borrow a chain saw. How bad is it under your part?"

"Mine's a tow truck special." She snapped a final view of the driver's side front wheel well. When she straightened, she touched the driver's door, turned, and inspected Dave. His hair, pushed straight back from his face and weighted by rain, pressed close to his scalp, giving the look of an adventurer to him. His white dress shirt lay translucent in the moisture. It molded against his skin outlining the muscles she'd glimpsed once before. The same ones which returned during brief hours of sleep ever since. She swirled her tongue, hunting for moisture in an arid mouth. She looked down, shook her head in a futile attempt to banish the image. He remained too close to the case even off the suspect list. She needed to remain objective. "I'm going inside. Get started on phone calls."

He threw a short broken branch low and fast toward the dumpster area. "After your calls, we could find a restaurant with electric service. Later, we could drive over and pick up the chainsaw. Interested?"

"Dr. Holmes. Are you suggesting a date?"

"Kindness. I heard someplace it eased interactions between neighbors."

****

"I'll be over there." Larry rubbed his knee with one hand and pointed at a padded bench with the other.

Sandra sent concern with her nod and eased away to the next enlarged photo.

He sighed. An hour ago, he'd arrived at Sandra's as the tornado sirens began wailing. They'd waited out the worst of the weather in her windowless bathroom watching storm reports on a small TV. At least the weather settled down to simple rain after the main storm.

Art Museum. It wasn't his first suggestion of a place to go on Friday night, but Sandra wanted to see this special exhibit. It contained several interesting things, more than he'd expected from the title— *Photographic History of Missouri.* He stretched out his legs and studied the jumbo picture in front of him.

"Kansas City rail yards, 1888." He mouthed the caption memorized a minute ago. It was a good scene. Strong lines. The tracks ran at shallow angles, crossed, and then appeared parallel. *Looks familiar. Recent.* He closed his eyes and concentrated on designs with almost straight lines. Was it the scoring on Betty's Easter ham? No, he could almost feel his hand holding a knife and drawing lines in a hurry. What sort of surface? He shook his head. He didn't want to think about it. The design might have been lines in the flowerbed left by his hand tools.

He studied the photo and found memories of his grandfather, a railroad man. The old man's career began years after the photo on the wall and included the great conversion from coal to diesel fuel. Decades ago, when he and Betty were children, he told them stories of checking the freights and directing the hobos away from the switching areas.

"Find something you like?" Sandra joined him on the bench in a puff of lilacs.

He relaxed in the sweet scent. "You smell special good tonight. New perfume?"

"New bottle of Lilac Breeze. You say the nicest things as you change the topic."

He laughed, glanced around at the other museum patrons, and pointed. "Trains."

She patted his arm. "It's too large for your living room. And your budget."

"How would you know my budget?"

"I've got a general idea of warehouse labor wages. No house payment—taxes and repairs make up your expenses there. Not many in AA have bulging savings accounts." She ticked the items off on her fingers. "Fine art isn't in my budget either."

"Don't suppose it is." He laced his fingers with hers. Their hands matched in an odd sort of way. His skin contained more fine little scars that caught the dirt and held it, but they shared the feature of strong fingers on working hands. He liked the look of combined strength. Delicate, fragile women never appealed to him. Sandra was vigorous—like Barbara. He blinked his way out of the quicksand of getting past and present confused again. Comparing the women wasn't fair to Sandra.

"Do you like trains well enough to ride one?" She faced the photo.

He shrugged. Playing tourist and traveling weren't for him. It was going on thirty years now since he'd seen the need to go more than eighty miles or so from the city center. "Might, if I wanted to take a trip bad enough. You planning one?"

"Nothing definite. Joseph suggested I take the train to Kansas City if I visit. He doesn't trust my car for the drive."

"Nothing's wrong with your car. Then again…" He shrugged. "I'm staying out of conflict between you and your son." He clenched his free hand at the memory of his behavior with Dave at the restaurant. The timing was bad. He knew ahead of time but went and set the date anyway. It still nagged at him for the doctor, son of an alcoholic, to see him in the afterglow of a binge. At least, the man showed the good sense and manners not to mention it at his apartment a few days later. The second meeting wasn't his idea at all. Sandra insisted on stopping at Dave's place without calling first.

He rubbed his knee again and shivered at the memory of Detective Morgan last Sunday afternoon. She looked startled, but either through training or natural acting ability she recovered in a few heartbeats. His hand squeezed his joint. He'd never been much of an actor. His shock at seeing her made it impossible to breathe normal until she was out of sight. *Maybe it was wrong to write the letter.*

"You hurting?" Sandra reached over and touched his wrist.

"Banged into a table leg today. Expect I'll be colorful tomorrow."

"You better be careful. Are any of your pills blood thinners?"

He imagined his pill bottles lined up on the kitchen table. Stomach, nerves, depression, blood pressure, and…he couldn't remember right off but blood thinner didn't sound right for either of the others. He stood and guided her up beside him. "Not that I remember."

"All your medicine worries me, Lawrence."

"Don't see why. You're not the one taking it. Or paying for it." He steered her into the adjoining room where a group of American landscapes hung in simple frames.

When the first announcement of closing time came

over the speakers, Larry urged her away from a small fish sculpture. "I hear our cue to leave. Do you want to stop for coffee and pie on the way home?"

"A great idea." She licked her lips.

Larry chuckled. Sandra suited his style. He liked knowing where he stood with a person, and she didn't hesitate to express her feelings. Keeping company with her enabled him to dream again. It gave him hope for steady companionship. Over dessert tonight he'd ask her to meet his sister, the next step on making Sandra a permanent part of his life.

A dream delayed could still be a dream fulfilled. At least that's how he understood the message in the current batch of psychology self-help books. For an instant, he imagined Sandra across the breakfast table day after day. No cheating on the whiskey, he thought. Having her around might even make it easier.

He almost stumbled on the last step as another modern proverb came to mind. *Justice delayed is still justice.*

****

Dave wiped au jus from his chin. "Did you say you gamble? I don't usually picture law enforcement placing bets."

"Let me repeat. We place all sorts of wagers within the family." Maylee adjusted the straw in her root beer. "Winning tends to be bragging rights."

"But not always?"

"No. It's been known for the loser to get a dirty household job or pick up a restaurant bill. More pride than money at stake."

He nodded, studied her eyes for a moment, and forced his gaze away. More than a casual glance at her lips sent the skin across his shoulders dancing in anticipation. He recalled the soft smoothness of the little patch of skin he'd tested behind her ear. Would her lips be softer? Sweeter? Would they be flavored with salt and root beer? "Sounds familiar. My brother Joe and our two cousins always tried to best each other at one thing or the other."

"Did you win?" She widened her lips into a full smile for an instant.

"My share. Since I ranked third in the quartet my odds edged out the ones you handled." He pushed away an incident where Joe ended up blamed for one of their larger flouts of authority. Had he gone back and helped him re-rake and bag the leaves they'd all scattered?

"I managed."

"Yes, I can see how you would."

The server placed the folder containing the bill beside Dave, and Maylee grabbed for it.

"Whoa." He lowered his hand over hers and blinked at the pleasure of skin-to-skin contact. "You're the guest. I'm the one who insisted we find a place with real dishes and waitresses."

"I've been employed long enough to have received a paycheck. You?"

"Now, you've been investigating clinic paydays. Is there anything a man can keep secret from you?" He rubbed her wrist with two fingers. "At least let me get the tip. A man needs to salvage a little pride."

She nodded and slid the folder to her portion of the table.

"Just to be clear, next time is my treat." His little invisible beast, Apprehension, poked his head out of the not-yet-digested meal and stared in disbelief. There would be another time? Dave voluntarily planned to spend non-running minutes near a handgun? Knowingly? "Need to make any stops on our way home?"

She sighed. "No thanks. My previous plans are in shambles."

A few moments later he held the restaurant door for her. "Let me guess. You planned a run in the rain followed by an evening drive."

"Shoe shopping."

He unlocked his car and gazed into her eyes while holding her door. Serious rather than the humor highlights which visited during their dinner conversation reflected back at him. Mrs. Gossen commented on Maylee's shoes today. Dressy, instead of practical. She dressed in suit, black hose, and heels for the funeral. His skin temperature threatened to flare out of control at the memory of her skirt sliding along her perfect legs as she relocated and squatted while taking photos. It proved to be a good thing to take a few minutes to change into dry clothes. He lowered his gaze past jeans which only hinted at her sculpted legs until he reached red cross trainers, same as she'd worn in the park. "You've a few miles left on those."

"Emphasis on few. Are you familiar with the Poppy Run?"

"Should I be?" He hurried around and slipped into the driver's seat.

"The Poppy Run raises funds for disabled veterans' organizations. This year the funds are designated to expand a van service."

"When?" He shifted his gaze away from her smooth hands on the seat belt.

"Sunday of Memorial Day weekend."

"Name your shoe store. May as well give you a full two weeks to break them in."

"Don't worry about it. I'll get them tomorrow—after I pick up the rental."

"Are you sure? I may never offer to take you shopping again." He shook his head and disguised it as checking traffic. The only shopping he enjoyed was of the farmer's market variety. The mix of sweet fruit, dirt clinging to root vegetables, and tangy spice from a food stand combined to heighten all his senses and desire to linger. Shoes, clothes, and home furnishings were purchased as walk in, pull off the shelf, and find a cashier items.

"Tomorrow," she repeated. "I'm running the 10K, the shoes will be fine. It isn't as if I'll be running tonight. Want to sponsor me?"

"Depends. Website I can check?"

"Affirmative. Poppyrunstl dot com. As of early last week the 10K and marathon weren't filled."

He rolled an immature idea around in his head. Two full weeks to train. If the weather—and the clinic workload—cooperated, it was doable. It might be a good thing to run toward a goal instead of away from the past. "Sounds promising. Not the marathon. I'd need to find a cardiologist at the mid-point."

Chapter Eleven

Tinkling wind chimes and distant laughter banished the silence between Dave and Sandra as they reached the base of the curved ramp. The Missouri Botanical Garden hosted hundreds of visitors this Mother's Day afternoon. The large grounds enabled the family groups to find space. He gestured toward a fountain surrounded by benches, the grouping inviting quiet conversation.

Dave eased down beside Sandra and traced the curve of the wooden bench arm. He welcomed a few minutes to sit after walking through the formal gardens closer to the main gate. This small patio occupied one entrance to the home garden and demonstration area, a favorite with both of them. The vegetable beds across a small lawn featured small plants poking out in rows to break up an expanse of fine dirt today, but the pansies added a cheerful note to the walkway borders. "Nice spot. Are you having a good Mother's Day?"

"No complaint." She smiled before taking a deep breath. "I like the garden. A visit is a treat."

He leaned against the armrest and nodded assent. Today he escorted a very agreeable but quiet Sandra. During their brunch she'd chatted about her neighbors and co-workers without her typical sudden leaps from topic to topic. Since their arrival in the gardens she'd talked little and looked thoughtful often. Was she making an important decision? He expected the impulsive Sandra to jump out of her body at any moment. "Nice fountain. Three little bronze rascals looking for trouble."

"And finding it. Raccoons. Have you ever been close to real ones?"

"I dragged fresh road kill out of the traffic lane once. Impressive teeth. I made sure to not get involved. Animators skip over a few things when putting them in movies with happy forest scenes."

"Sam took me hunting. Once." She unzipped her fanny pack and poked among the contents.

"When? I can't remember you going hunting." He held clear memories of his dad and a friend going two or three times every fall. He'd asked to go along several times, but in a rare show of agreement, his parents told him he needed to wait until age twelve. By then…well, the world had changed for him. Hunting didn't enter conversations when touching a gun generated cold sweats and trembling instead of symbolizing manhood and independence.

"It was a long time ago—a year or two before you were born." She dabbed a tissue below her nose. "Allergies."

Continue. Stories from Sandra including Sam appeared seldom and ended too short for a man to learn details of his father. Maybe this hunting experience would reveal when and where she'd learned to handle—or rather, mis-handle—grandpa's revolver.

"Four of us went into the woods an hour after sunset. Plus Jim's two hounds. I guess the dogs knew their job. I spent most of my time tripping over roots and rocks in the dark. By the time the dogs treed the first critter my flashlight was fading. Jim's girl and I found our way back to the truck and spent the next two hours waiting for the men."

"Did they shoot any?"

"Four. Jim skinned them out when he got home. Later, he sold the pelts to a dealer. They're not good meat." She pulled out a cigarette and looked around for signs forbidding her habit. "One night. My entire hunting career."

Dave straightened as the old fear danced on his spine. Sandra may have only hunted coon one night. She didn't handle a gun then. Had she ever practiced? Or had he witnessed her first, only, and deadly shot years later? The question she avoided answering every time he asked teetered on the tip of his tongue before tumbling out. "Why? Why not divorce Dad?"

She inspected the smoke in her hand as if she'd never seen one before. "It's complicated. You don't need to know."

"You're answering as if I'm still a kid. I'm an adult now." He stared into her faded blue eyes. "I stopped in Marshall last month and read the file."

"Then you already know."

"The reports have the facts. Words and pictures filled in details of the 'what.' They don't explain everything." A shiver skimmed across his shoulders at mention of the photos. The collection of colored images showed more detail and added to the unwelcome dreams that still visited. The kitchen with white cabinets and floral curtains looked the same. The difference was obvious—Sam Holmes' body collapsed on the floor. He blinked away the photo that haunted him the most—the lilac print of the back door curtain spattered with blood.

He touched her wrist. "The official records neither confirm nor deny if Sam was having an affair. Even then, why not a divorce?"

"I believed the worst of him." She flicked her lighter as a nervous gesture, well away from the cigarette. "Turned out he did stop off for a drink with his shift the nights he came home late. Weekends," she shrugged. "He picked up a few handyman jobs on the side. I didn't find out he was telling the truth until later…after I got stupid."

Dave waited. Water splashed around the sculptures and a family came by, three children chattering in excited voices breaking the bubble of serious around the bench.

"Enough." Sandra put the cigarette away and exchanged it for a stick of gum. "I'm worried about Lawrence."

"Is he seeing another woman? Involved in illegal activity?" Dave recalled Larry's pale face during hasty introductions a week ago.

"No signs of your first option. It's…well, in the other direction. The other night he got too close to mentioning marriage. I'm not interested. I tried it. It didn't work." She folded the gum wrapper into a tiny square. "Don't need to tell you how it ended."

He gripped the smooth bench arm. His parents' marriage ended in front of him. What he wanted to know, the topic she avoided, were events of days, weeks, or even months climaxed on one tragic hot August night. "I remember the final event." *Too vivid. Too often.* He cleared his throat and switched subjects. "Was Larry ever married?"

"He's never mentioned a wife." She studied her nails for a long moment. "Girlfriends have ended up in the conversation a few times. I don't ask for names or numbers. He's a good person. I'd like to keep him as a friend. I want to meet his sister. But I like my privacy. You know I do."

Privacy. Quiet. Control. Since her return to St. Louis, Sandra maintained walls around certain aspects of life. She insisted on the very things forbidden to prisoners. He gazed at her hands moving restless against her waist pack and tried to ignore the similarities between mother and son in the long, strong fingers. "Then why are you worried?"

"His health. David, the man gets a new prescription every couple of weeks. He takes more pills in a day than I do in a month."

He got comfortable with one ankle resting on a knee. Unless things had changed during the last month, Sandra took very little medicine. The previous time the topic came up between them she admitted to only a multivitamin and one blood pressure medication daily. "And you know this because…?"

"We went out for breakfast a few weeks ago. He brought his morning medicine with him. I tell you, he took six pills. Then tells me he has more in the evening."

"Did he say what they were for?"

"Here's the problem." She tapped one foot. "I asked. He claimed not to know. Oh, he pointed to one and said 'blood pressure' and another for 'nerves.' He was too vague for my comfort. Can you talk to him?"

"It's not my business. He should talk to his own doctor."

"He's got two or three."

Dave detected worry in her eyes in addition to her voice. Sandra seldom showed this much concern for her biological family. Did she actually care for Larry deeper than she was admitting? Or did her relatives, including him, keep the self-preservation fence around Sandra too tall? "Suggest he pick one, take in all his medications, and find out if they interact with each other."

"You make it sound simple."

He realized he'd described a world where patients followed directions. Larry might not. Recovering alcoholics knew how to lie. And his eyes and deliberate hand movements the first time they met indicated more than a mild stomach virus. This situation had potential to be complex. He could think of half a dozen places for the straightforward solution to go awry. A person dare not forget Sandra's personality either. Suggestions came out of her mouth sounding identical to harsh commands. Larry might ignore her. Or the physician who reviewed the medications could find justification in their use.

"Enough of my problems." She tucked the tiny square of wrapper into her pack and stood. "Now tell me about your neighbor while we walk over to the Japanese Garden."

"Mrs. Gossen? Why are you interested in a retired widow? I believe she already has a favorite hairdresser."

"I'm referring to the girl you introduced in the parking lot."

"Maylee. She works for the city." He shaded the truth in neutral colors, aware Sandra would take any positive words and expand them in an invisible matchmaking kettle.

"She didn't wear rings."

"Have you taken to checking the hands at every introduction?" He couldn't stop a small smile as he recalled an image of Maylee dressed for work. The only jewels involved happened to be small pearl earrings that played peek-a-boo in her hairstyle. If he needed to describe her appearance in one word he'd pick "practical" while "feminine" floated in a close second. The memory of her body in his arms—for one brief moment—warmed his neck more than today's sunshine. It was the other thing—her hardware—that bothered him.

"You should ask her out."

"It's not simple." A shiver skipped across his shoulders. Friday's supper in a busy casual restaurant and stop at the mall left his good sense to leave her alone wrestling with hormones reined in too long. Even prompting her to talk about the funeral didn't lessen the urge to give her a proper kiss.

"David. When did you become shy around good-looking girls?"

When they started carrying guns.

****

Maylee parked in front of her childhood home and counted the vehicles in the driveway. Two SUVs, one sub-compact, and a full-size pickup truck gleamed in afternoon sunshine. All of the Morgan brothers appeared to be present. No doubt they'd been visiting for hours. The only question now concerned how many were checking the street for her arrival.

It wasn't the Mother's Day celebration they

planned. Yes, Dianne insisted on hosting her own party. The Morgan tradition since the oldest moved out of the house including attending church together before invading their childhood home for a large brunch and boisterous games.

This year, Maylee's work schedule initiated a series of early morning calls rescheduling the family meal to an early supper. She retrieved a grocery sack with three bottles of juice, adjusted her invisible shield against sibling barbs, and entered the house.

"Happy Mother's Day." She pulled Dianne into a hug the instant the bags settled on the floor. Familiar scents of cinnamon, sausage, and hot coffee multiplied the comfort of her mother's arms. "Sorry I'm late. Work."

"We need to talk." Dianne eased back a small step and held Maylee at arm's length.

Maylee stared into her mother's face and absorbed a dozen silent question marks. "I can't say anything about an on-going investigation. You know the rules."

"Confidentiality. Don't overuse it, daughter."

Tom tells me the opposite. "After an arrest, then I can say more." Growing up as the daughter of an assistant and then elected county prosecutor rubbed the rules of confidentiality into every member of the Morgan family early in life.

Dianne tipped her head and examined her daughter head to toe and back again. "Can you tell me why two officers came here, to my home, to collect paperwork from 2001?"

"It's related to a case."

"Be careful, Maylee. Not all your father's correspondence is from admirers."

"I know. My partner's not letting me read it." She pressed her lips tight to forbid her sigh to escape. Tom espoused conflict of interest to keep her eyes off certain portions of potential evidence. Mixed in with his professionalism she'd spotted a little concern identical to the love and caution in her mother's eyes. "It's not a secret in this house Dad stepped on toes and made enemies through the years."

"Public record." Dianne pulled a clear plastic pitcher out of a cabinet. "His opponents managed to put everything except our pillow talk into the media."

"We didn't request gossip." She wanted to comfort her mother, erase any old wounds that may have opened again when the officers and their subpoena arrived. Some things a daughter couldn't do. But she could keep silent about the recent letters until this case was solved. And after? No reason to worry a parent after the fact either.

Letters. A shiver rippled down her spine. A second anonymous threat arrived in Friday's mail and waited in the mailbox until she collected it with the other pieces Saturday morning. Friday evening, her routine, including dealing with correspondence, had shattered due to the storm, insurance calls, power outage, and Dave. *A most unusual neighbor.* She called on her meager acting skill to disguise the curiosity threatening to overtake her. Her mother was too observant to allow thoughts of him to display. Let the family think storm damage to her car the only distraction.

The day they removed Dave Holmes from the suspect list, she gained the freedom to get acquainted. An hour, closer to two, in his company Friday evening and she'd discovered he contained more layers than

Dianne's finest chocolate cake. He chauffeured her to supper unaware how his shaggy, damp hair tempted her fingers to reach out and touch, arrange, sample. She remembered the conversation in the chain restaurant down to the mild argument over the check. It was a good thing she tossed out a question about Christmas before they arrived at the shoe store. He'd visibly relaxed while talking about the different holiday customs at the mission hospital.

"Hey, Sis." Matt, the youngest of the Morgan brothers, swept into the room. Their grinning nephew, Steve's youngest, dangled from his arm.

"What a charming couple you make. Let me guess. Uncle Matt's a magnet and you're a nail."

"King Kong." Tyler shook his head. "Must stop. Save Trade Center One."

She looked up at the ceiling. Reminders of September 11, 2001, popped up everywhere.

"Enough." Matt pried Tyler's fingers off his bicep and let the boy drop the final inches to the kitchen floor. "Go. Save the world from your father."

"Yes, sir." Tyler hurried out the door.

"Nice ride out front. Care to explain?" Matt crossed his arms and stared at Maylee.

"You noticed. What do you think of the color? Official name is Alien 2. Don't go calling it a military modifier of green with small boys around." She stared into his hazel eyes in her best family championship form. All of the siblings engaged in staring contests, but she and Matt were tied for the championship. She blinked first. "It's a rental. Another one of the act of God sort of accidents."

"I'm listening."

"As you may recall, it stormed Friday. A tree near my parking spot decided to take a nap on my Camry. Enough detail?"

"Totaled?"

"I'll find out tomorrow. Wheels of the World is holding it in temporary custody." She turned away and began filling the pitcher with ice and juice. "Tell me about your universe. Did you kick butt this week?"

"All things posterior are under control. New class doesn't start until next Monday so I wrangled an extra day off base."

"Lucky you." She stopped, before her lips betrayed her suspicion that Matt drove up from Fort Leonard Wood to see a mystery girl, as much as family. She liked the idea of her brother with a sweetheart. Matt's dating status would deflect questions away from her. The detective portion of her personality wanted a name. The sister would settle for knowing an occupation or a little background on which to base an opinion.

"Want an assist looking for your next car?"

She exaggerated her shrug. "Do you have a line on an armored personnel carrier?"

Chapter Twelve

Larry climbed off the forklift and tugged on the end of the charging cord. One instant of resistance, a short jerk, and the retractable reel released the insulated wire. He jabbed the end into the heavy-duty charger and watched until the indicator light came to life with an orange glow.

"Last call for mandatory employee meeting."

"Ask me if I care." Larry muttered a reply to the unfamiliar voice on the overhead speaker. He tucked his gloves in his back pocket and followed Jim, the other forklift driver, toward the lunch and meeting room.

A minute later, Larry walked into a babble of voices. Every stackable fiberglass chair in the small, tidy room was taken. An additional half dozen chairs from the public reception room narrowed the aisle on the far side. The table stood folded up against the far wall and already one person leaned against the fridge. He followed Jim to a span of wall space, and they each claimed a piece.

He reached down and rubbed his knee. A chair sure would be welcome. He scanned for an overlooked empty. Nothing. Why's the second shift here?

"Excuse me." A young man dressed for the assembly room bumped Larry's shoulder as he pulled off his hairnet and stuffed it in a pocket.

Larry shrugged. "They tell you anything?"

"No more than usual. You think we'll finally get the truth of the rumors?"

Larry rested his head against painted cinder block wall. Facts would be good. The whispers of the company being for sale, closing down, or buying out a similar sized competitor grew louder by the week. At lunch and breaks the employees presented and denied snatches of overheard conversation. Old Mr. Yates was retiring. Young Yates intended to expand. After an especially lively debate during lunch last week, he'd job hunted most of an evening on a web site. He didn't like what he found. Warehouse and light vehicle jobs were scarce. And almost all of them required a commute out of the city, deep into Jefferson or St. Charles counties.

Silence skimmed over the room as the company owner entered.

Larry straightened and squared his shoulders against the wall. He liked Mr. Yates. The small man knew his business and the employees. A couple times a week he walked rounds through warehouse, assembly, and packaging areas, staying familiar with the work and the employees. But he was a dozen years past normal retirement age.

Larry crossed his arms and looked for the younger Yates, a nephew included in several of last month's rumors. *Not here.* He glanced at Jim.

"Your attention, please." Mr. Yates closed the door behind a young stranger in a black suit. "Today, we put the rumors to rest. Officially, as of noon today, Yates Distributing no longer exists. After a nice long run of forty-five years, I've sold the firm to Reed and White

Distribution."

Larry stared at the man beside Mr. Yates. *Doesn't look old enough to shave.*

"Never heard of them," Jim whispered from his right.

"Listen up." Mr. Yates quelled the growing mutterings. "Earned vacation and sick leave will be paid. Every person here has an opportunity to apply and interview for your same or similar position in the new company." He set his hand on the shoulder of the taller, younger man. "Allow me to introduce Mr. Brannon, St. Louis manager for Reed and White Distribution. He'll give you an overview and answer questions. You'll also each receive an information packet as you leave the meeting."

Mr. Brannon launched into his first paragraph of company history.

What's he saying? Larry rubbed his ear at the unfamiliar accent. He looked at a few of his co-workers and they appeared confused also. Did he say Springfield, Massachusetts? Couldn't Mr. Yates get a fair deal in the Midwest?

"All of the St. Louis operations will be relocated to the Earth City facility. The exact future of this building is still under discussion. It will no longer be used for any of the current functions. Timeframe for the move will have relocation to the St. Louis County buildings complete by the end of this month. Questions?"

"Will everyone get rehired?" A woman in the second row sounded worried.

"Do the people already at Earth City need to reinterview?"

"Can we use a real paper application? Computer

forms and the like make me nervous."

Larry swallowed down a cluster of impulsive words gathering on the root of his tongue. Other employees, several of them at a difficult age to find new work, continued to voice many of the questions he gathered in his brain. He needed to keep a job. He glanced around at the others and calculated his odds. The result sent a shiver down his spine. The same fear crawled back up again when Mr. Brannon informed them the total workforce would be cut by one-third.

"Hey," Jim whispered. "How about we read those packets over lunch at Tina's?"

Larry nodded. Tina's Diner, two blocks away was a safe place. He could drink ice water, eat a sandwich, and share his honest opinion of Mr. Fresh Face. He tuned in to the questions and answers again, editing out the extra letters in the new manager's heavy Boston accent.

Half an hour later, Larry crowded into a booth with Jim and two other warehouse workers. He glanced around and counted ten other employees of Yates invading Tina's for lunch. Actually, they'd all been dismissed until regular shift tomorrow. "I don't look forward to driving out to Earth City every day. Not interested in the unemployment line either."

"I heard Midwest Cartage is hiring. Maybe I'll shine up my permits and go back to over-the-road. Wife won't like it. Money's okay." Jim sighed before turning his attention to the server.

Larry ordered soup and grilled cheese to go with his soda. The meeting may have sorted out the rumors, but it started a headache deep at the base of his brain. "We're getting too old to change jobs. All of us." He glanced at the other three around the table. "How close to retirement are you, Rich?"

"Seven years, give or take." He shrugged and continued, "Might try auto body again. All the mechanic stuff I used to do got outdated with computers and sealed units."

"Interviews start tomorrow." Bill slipped papers out of his large white envelope. "Man, the new manager looked young. If I worked a bar I'd check his ID twice. When did we get old and worn out?"

Larry agreed in silence. Three years with Yates. His attendance was good. *Gotten smart enough to take a vacation day after Paul visits.* At evaluations last year, he'd received the same raise as the others in the warehouse. And now this. In one short meeting his plans to replace his truck later this year dried up and blew away like a dead leaf.

What would he tell Betty? Nothing, until she forced the issue. His sister still held the crazy notion he should get on with a landscape and maintenance firm. Only last month she'd mentioned their distant cousin and how he would welcome Larry to his business. Working out in the extreme heat and cold of St. Louis didn't appeal to him. If it came to one or the other—he'd commute to Earth City.

He ate, supplied a stray word or two to the conversation, and worried. The other men at the table had working wives, a second income to keep a roof over their heads. He owned a home—a house without a mortgage—and a bank balance which refused to grow.

Sandra? He chewed his sandwich and recalled her face when he'd hinted at marriage after the Art Museum visit. Her smile faded the longer he talked of living together in his home. What did he have to offer her now?

He swallowed the last spoonful of soup. His final wisp of hope to get Sandra to share his life slid down with it.

****

"Thank you." Maylee disconnected the call and sighed.

"Get the verdict on your car?" Tom looked up from a stack of letters on the table.

She pushed one hand through her hair and nodded. "It's beyond all hope. I need to remember to snag an empty box or two on my way out tonight. I may as well pick up the last of my captive personal belongings on my way home."

"You could get Doctor Handsome to assist you."

She swallowed down the rude noise climbing her throat. She'd not seen him since their supper on Friday. Mrs. Gossen, however, had waylaid her late yesterday with thirty minutes of narrative and questions. "Anything in the letters?"

"Not yet. I'll give you good grades for changing the topic."

"We're at work. My trainer cautioned me to stay focused on the case." She looked out their fourth floor window and recited the cross streets as the view changed from rebounding downtown to shabby. For an instant, while moving her gaze back to the work she'd suspended for the personal phone call, her focus stalled on the side-by-side photos of the remaining suspects.

Tony looks less likely than ever. The information Johnson picked up from the conversation at the visitation didn't lead any further than the charity. It

149

turned out to be a legitimate Catholic organization. The main function of Children of the Far Hills turned out to be staffing and supporting medical facilities in Central and South America. The Saterros had given generously of money and time to the charity for more than a dozen years. Maylee recalled Tony's large, strong hands, and shivered. "And with that said…I'll get back to the Saterro boxes."

The day before the world changed. Maylee let the phrase from the first letter stay front and center in her brain. Coupled with the references to her father, the detectives agreed the writer meant September 11, 2001, as the day of change. As a result, they now combed through accident and crime reports beginning forty-eight-hours prior to the first plane striking the World Trade Center.

Tom hummed a disconnected collection of Beatles tunes as he reviewed correspondence from Gary Morgan's home and office. The items from the home fit into one medium-sized shoe box. Dianne Morgan didn't get sentimental about the stray work-related letter directed to their home address. In general, the only items of paperwork she preserved longer than ten years consisted of copies of filed tax forms and check registers filled out in a rainbow of ink colors.

Maylee shuddered at one of Tom's particularly off-key phrases from "Hey, Jude" and picked up the next letter. Unlike her mother, the Saterros were pack rats of the highest order. During the initial search of the house the police discovered dozens of bankers boxes filled with household financial records, greeting cards, and correspondence. Organized and labeled with beginning and ending months, the stash filled the closet in the home office and then continued to a dozen stacked boxes against the wall. Initially, the detectives brought in one year of records to comb for possible threats against the late doctor. Yesterday, they'd returned with a warrant and a van to collect everything from September 2001 forward.

Have you confessed? Maylee double-checked the date on the paper in her hand. November 18, 2001. She read further into the letter before speaking. "I've got a reference to a traffic accident from an angry man. Signed it 'the lesser half of your victim.' Language gets religious in the final paragraph."

"Lesser half?" Tom closed the file in front of him.

"What do we know about Dr. Saterro's accident of September 10?"

"Not enough. City of Webster Groves issued a ticket. He paid a fine and lived through a license suspension of…six months." Tom turned back to a previous page of handwritten notes.

"What if?" Maylee opened her computer to the official accident report and then started pulling up files for the second driver, Marie B. Trudeau. "The woman died ten hours after the crash."

Tom read the next lines over her shoulder. "Marital status listed as single, parents as next of kin. She may have been married previous. Or engaged. Would an ex-husband or boyfriend wait all this time?"

"It's too soon to tell. The cemetery records make a connection to the particular discovery site." She clicked one of the other files to the top. "M. B. Trudeau is the second to last interred in the Galati plot. Grave was closed September 18, 2001. Payment made by Phillip Trudeau. Her father?"

Tom nodded and reached for the mouse. "Try the DMV records for a name change."

She read the letter again and drew a mental highlight over "lesser half." What sort of person reversed the way her grandfather joked about his wife?

****

Dave tapped on the hospital room door and pushed it open without waiting. He trusted the nurse two steps behind him to check the IV pump and focused on the man in the bed. He studied the patient's weathered skin and steel gray hair contrasting with the white linens a long moment before he realized the empty visitor chair stood pushed against the far wall.

"Wha…oh…" Pain crossed the elderly man's face as he drew a deep breath. He glanced at the nurse and then steadied his gaze at Dave. "Who are you? I don't remember you."

"Dr. Holmes." He gripped the patient's left hand, leaving the one with the IV undisturbed. "I'm the surgeon. We didn't meet until after the high-powered painkillers took effect. Tell me what you do remember, Mr. Trudeau."

"All in a mist. My sister brought me to emergency. I hurt powerful. All of it," he gestured to his groin.

"Yes, I imagine it did." Dave recalled his first sight of Mr. Trudeau when the man attempted to stifle groans during a pre-surgical exam. "Where is your sister?"

"Home." He grasped the bed rail. "Back in the morning."

"In this case, you get the story first." Dave hid a little disappointment behind a quick smile. Family members tended to ask more questions and prod him into using less technical language than patients surfacing from anesthesia.

"Hernia, I remember the first doc telling me before any medicine."

"Let me tell you what happened." Dave began one of the world's shorter speeches about strangulated hernias and their repair. He flicked his gaze to his patient's eyes often as he spoke and hunted for shorter words when they reflected confusion. These layman explanations challenged him almost as much as manipulating the tissues into position before repair. It reminded him of his weakness with patients—education.

Mr. Trudeau reached for the water glass, missed, and sighed. "Thirsty."

Dave stopped his narrative and loosened the sheet on the side of the bed while the nurse poured fresh water and held the glass.

"Tired." Mr. Trudeau waved the drink away after one sip.

"This won't take long. I prefer to check now to prevent a problem later." Dave inspected the dressing. It looked exactly as it should four hours post-surgery. "We'll release you tomorrow morning. Your sister said you live together?"

"Since she was widowed."

"Good. The social worker will give you information for home care visits and schedule your first post-op visit to the clinic. And I'll check on you early, before breakfast." He pulled the sheet above the patient's waist but left it loose on the side.

"Doc?" Mr. Trudeau raised the hand with the IV tube. "How long will I be on this leash?"

"Until the bag hanging up there is gone. Three

hours give or take. Are you hungry?"

"A little."

"The nurses ordered you a special tray from dietary. You slept through regular supper service." Dave pulled a penlight from his coat pocket and leaned forward. "Now let me guide your chin for a minute and take a closer look at your eyes."

"Where are my glasses? I'm near blind without them."

"Turn a little. There. All done." Dave nodded at the nurse.

"We kept them safe." The nurse removed glasses with thick lenses from the nightstand, gave them a quick polish with a tissue, and eased them on Mr. Trudeau's face. "How does the doc look now?"

"Better. Less blur."

Dave concentrated on the bedside computer keyboard for an instant before entering an order for oral antibiotics. He glanced over his shoulder at three raps on the door. "Maybe your supper's here." He raised his voice. "Enter."

Dave blinked away surprise. When the door swung open it wasn't an aide bringing the patient's delayed supper. Maylee advanced into the room two paces ahead of her partner. What interest did the police have with his patient? Didn't they belong in emergency? Their questions should be for a post gunshot or accident victim. "Do you have the right room?"

"Mr. Phillip Trudeau?" Maylee paused at the foot of the bed and displayed her badge. "We're detectives, and we have a few questions for you."

"Excuse us." Dave stepped to the far corner of the room and beckoned her to follow. He dropped his voice to a whisper, hoping his patient's hearing did not compensate for poor sight. "Why are you here?"

"We have questions for Mr. Trudeau."

I have a few of my own. He sealed his lips against the first words gathering at the back of his tongue. What connection did his elderly patient have to any police case? And where had she been this weekend? Busy? Or avoiding him?

If she'd expressed such interest in his patients on Friday, he'd talked more in jargon and relayed experiences without names. Then again, when he looked at her he didn't think incisions, vital signs, or drug dosages. He glanced at her partner, Wilson, exchanging a few quiet words with the nurse. At least, the male detective's face wore a coating of apology. "You always talk in questions."

Did she snicker at him? He stacked his arms across his chest, fighting the urge to lean closer for a stronger sample of the tropical flower scent wafting from her hair. He needed to give a wider berth to her weapon. Why did they allow police handguns in the building? "Well?"

She glanced toward the elderly man. Mr. Trudeau faced the nurse and pointed one finger in their direction. "Your defense of patients is admirable, Dr. Holmes."

"Be wary. He still has anesthetic in his system. Anything he says won't hold up in court. I'll swear to it, if necessary."

"Did you know you have an unique sunburn? It crawls up your neck without a speck of sunlight hitting it."

He ignored the heat on his skin, a hazard of pale complexions, and stared at her, silently counting the seconds. At sixteen she glanced away. *An expert.*

****

Maylee swung her gaze toward the trio of patient, nurse, and detective at the bedside. She needed a moment to gather her thoughts again. Hospitals, especially these higher, quieter floors brought back memories of watching her father die. In a room identical to this—two floors down.

She blinked twice, drew a deep breath, and longed to be in Mr. Trudeau's home, a chaotic emergency department, or Thompson's front porch. Anywhere but here—caught between unpleasant memories and a certain doctor with golden hair brushing the collar of his white coat and threatening to crack her confident shell.

The monitor on the IV stand beeped and flashed as Phillip reached out to shake Tom's hand. "Speak up, young man. Most people around here mumble."

"No music conducting." The nurse pushed the reset button and guided her patient's hand back to rest against the sheet.

"He's tired. Not thinking clearly." Dave's voice from a foot away claimed her attention.

She turned back to him and couldn't help but begin an inventory of his coat pocket—pen, flashlight, notepad…screwdriver? "We won't be long. Our question list is short this time."

"Unlike when you descend on a victim's co-workers?" He pulled his phone out and frowned at the screen.

She stiffened and stared into his face.

"Sorry. First impressions. They do stay the longest, remain the most difficult to erase."

"If you don't mind." She stepped away and took a place near Mr. Trudeau's left arm.

"I do mind. However, surgery is demanding my presence. Jenn." He shifted his attention to the nurse. "Please stay. You have my permission to rid the room of police if Mr. Trudeau shows signs of stress."

First impressions. The dominant image from her first meeting with him remained the sharpest. His hair was longer then, dancing between his shoulder blades as if a fit, lean barbarian ran to war along the park path. She blinked her focus back to the present.

"I'm Detective Morgan. My partner and I have a few questions for you." She held up a miniature audio recorder. "May we?"

Phillip Trudeau rolled his head on the pillow to look at her. "Police?"

"Yes. Nothing you've done." Tom waited for the door to close behind the doctor. "We're looking for a little information."

"Is it the neighborhood kids? Have they been spray painting garage doors again?" His voice tapered off as if he ran out of breath.

"No graffiti." Tom opened his notebook and wrote a line.

"We'd like to talk about your daughter." Maylee studied his face, flipping on her internal lie detector.

Phillip turned back to her with his forehead full of question wrinkles. "My daughter's dead. Years ago. Marie, sweet girl."

"Tell us about it." She touched his fragile skin.

"Auto accident. Her mother changed. Never laughed or sparkled the same. I try to forget, but it comes back. Holidays. Her birthday." He took a deep breath and froze his features in pain. "It hurts like the devil."

"Take your time, Mr. Trudeau."

"You've got a report. I don't think I can add anything. It's been too long for details."

"Tell us something about Marie." She circled her thumb on the back of his hand. "Did she have a lot of friends? A boyfriend?"

"She moved out of our house. Shared an apartment with a cousin. In Soulard." He separated his phrases and took slow, shallow breaths. "Friends from school. Her work. Both men and women."

"Did any of them contact you after the funeral?"

"Women from her work stopped over." He motioned for the water.

Maylee concentrated on the faint cleanser scent mixing with Mr. Trudeau's stale breath above the bed. "Anyone else?"

"A man. Claimed he loved her. Carried on like a widower. Upset we didn't list him in the obituary. Half a liar."

"What do you mean?" In her experience liars didn't come in half portions.

"He always used her other name. Barbara. She liked the variation of her middle name. Marie Beebe Trudeau."

"Were they engaged? Promised?"

Phillip shook his head. "He drank. Marie worried about his love of the bottle. And…she leaned toward taking orders."

"Orders?"

"Holy orders. Nun." Phillip squinted at her. "Missions. Children of the Far Hills."

"I understand," Tom injected. "Excuse my Protestant friend."

"Pest. Now, I think on it. He, the boyfriend, pushed until my wife and I visited a lawyer."

Tom glanced at Maylee long enough to indicate he'd do the next few. "What did he want?"

"Murder." Phillip closed his eyes and deflated. "He carried on saying the other driver should go to jail. No evidence. Marie got distracted sometimes. Police wrote the guy a ticket. I had a wife to console and a daughter to bury. No sense stirring up more problems."

"Where did you bury your daughter?" Tom leaned forward.

"Grandparents." His voice faded and he pointed to the water. After two sips through the straw while Maylee held the glass close, he adjusted his mouth to speak again. "All Saints. Her mother was a Galati."

"Do you remember his name? This pushy boyfriend."

Phillip worried the sheet with his fingers. "Larry. I think. Last name started with a T. Thomas? No. He had his membership at Joan of Arc." Phillip blinked at Maylee and the recorder running on the small table. "Are you done? The doc mentioned supper. Bet it's cold by now."

Chapter Thirteen

Larry took the last big swallow of his sweet soda to wash down two over-the-counter painkillers and an allergy tablet. *Tuesday isn't my day.* He belched, patted his stomach, and tossed the empty soda can into the recycle bag.

He pulled out his flip phone and hesitated. Did he know the right words to open a conversation with Sandra? She wanted to go tonight. A voice mail time stamped an hour ago confirmed her determination to make the meeting at Joan of Arc tonight. He could beg off with a headache. *Almost true.* He rubbed the base of his skull where tension from yesterday's announcement sat like a magnet. Darn thing pulled the questions on the new application and re-employment interview into a pile big enough to bring tears.

"A man needs an AA meeting most when he wants it least." He recited the line his sponsor liked to use.

A moment later he dialed Sandra. "Hi, sweetie. You ready?"

"Willing and able, Lawrence." She laughed at her own joke. "Are you feeling better today?"

He stared out his kitchen window and considered the question. Where was the relief he expected after the interview this afternoon? Did it stay caught in the web of words he'd presented all out of order and rambling to an impatient man from the Earth City facility? He considered telling her all, confessing his worries. An instant later he swallowed and painted the situation pretty for his best girl. "I'll manage. Safe to drive. Don't worry."

"See you in fifteen?"

"Yeah. I'm on my way." He halted the next word. Even as a younger man he made his attempts at declaring emotion in person. He grabbed a Cardinals cap on his way out the door.

He muttered to the empty cab as he drove toward Sandra's duplex. "Tomorrow. Wednesday they give us the verdict. They're doing it so fast I wonder if they had their minds made up before they started. I won't tell Sandra until then. No sense in getting her worried." He checked his mirror. "Streets are busy tonight. Is that black SUV following me?"

A few minutes later he leaned back and braced his hands on the iron porch railing at Sandra's side of a brick duplex. She promised to be ready "in a minute." Seconds, minutes, anything up to a quarter hour, were flexible things around her, not tied to the movement of watch hands. He glanced toward the street every few seconds and sighed relief when no dark SUVs rolled past.

I'm getting jumpy. He searched for another word, one more likely to be used by the college man conducting the warehouse interviews. Skittish? Paranoid? He should relax, enjoy the rest of the evening. Continued employment at Yates or Reed and White Distributing or whatever name the owner slapped on the building was out of his hands now. He didn't have any influence after he walked out of the back office at three fifteen.

"All set." Sandra crowded onto the tiny porch and paused to lock the door. "You're wearing a serious face. If you owned a dog, I'd suspect it died."

"Just thinking. Want to skip the meeting? Nice evening for a walk in the park."

"We missed Thursday. I need this. They showed too many beer commercials during the game last night."

"Meeting it is. We'll even be early. Time for coffee and a little visiting before things get serious." He shrugged and followed her off the porch. "Cards pulled it out during the last inning." He retrieved information from the radio spots and chatter at work. This early in the season he didn't watch many games. And last night, he struggled to remember what he did after work. Yes, he remembered now. He'd stayed at home, fretted about the scheduled interview, and polished half a dozen of the larger combat knives in his collection.

"I swear. The team makes me nervous this year." She led the way toward his truck.

Larry listened to Sandra chatter about her beauty shop clients as he drove. The second and third times he checked his mirrors a dark SUV trailed along two or three lengths behind. *Let's test this.*

"Where are you going?" Sandra reached for the assist grip handle as he turned on a small street at the last instant.

"Different route."

"Least you could do is use your turn signal."

He shrugged. Two blocks later he turned again. He worked his way toward the back of the church that hosted the Tuesday AA meeting. He swallowed hard with one block to go when what appeared to be the same dark SUV showed up behind him. He continued past the church parking lot.

"You missed it," she snapped. "Are you safe to drive? Did you mix up your pills?"

"Quiet. I know what I'm doing." He growled. A moment later he began to circle the block. He pulled into a parking spot on the street in front of the school entrance. "See, arrived in plenty of time."

"No thanks to a scenic tour." She opened the door and exited before he could get around to play the gentleman. An instant after her feet were firm on the asphalt, she slammed the truck door hard enough to rattle the screwdriver stored in the console.

"I've got my reasons. I've got important things on my mind tonight." He hurried beside her and held the door to the church annex. *My job's at risk.* He sealed his mouth against the words on his tongue.

"We can talk on the way home."

"Maybe." He scanned the faces in the meeting room. A stranger in new jeans and a polo shirt stood talking to Carl, their self-appointed leader. The posture and short hair made him guess the new man was recent military, a common thread in the groups.

Larry sat beside Sandra and occupied his hands with a paper cup of coffee when they formed their circle. Carl spoke first, he always did, and tonight his words washed over Larry without leaving a trace.

"Any introductions?"

"I'm Ed," the stranger replied. "Fellow at work told me about your group."

"Welcome." The greeting came as a chorus followed by first names from several members.

Larry nodded at Ed but didn't trust his voice with actual words. All the things he should have said during this afternoon's interview bubbled up, and he feared they would escape.

"Sandra." She stretched out her arm and leaned over two people to shake Ed's hand. "Ninety-five days and counting."

"Congratulations." Ed smiled at Sandra before shifting his gaze behind her.

"Not as long," Larry managed. Numbers swirled at the back of his throat. He wasn't going to tell the truth, not until he warned Sandra. The tally currently in use for the groups escaped him at the moment. Another number, much larger, the time span he implied around his sister tempted him. He looked down at the floor and gathered enough scattered sense to keep quiet. This business at work strode forward again. Couldn't the Eastern owners find a Midwesterner to manage the site? Someone who understood St. Louis' push and pull of race and region? *Do I really want to drive all the way to Earth City? I can't afford to lose the job. Honest work is hard to come by.*

He recoiled in surprise as Sandra brushed her fingers against his arm. A glance at the wall clock informed him he'd drifted for more than five minutes.

"Sorry," he whispered. "Bad couple days at work."

"Baked brownies today." She soothed.

Temptation lived in Sandra's baked goods. They were tasty as sin, but she'd serve them with questions across a small table. Tonight he didn't have the energy to either dodge them or keep the lies straight. "Another time."

"Your choice." She shrugged.

"I'll help with the chairs before I take you home." He stood and discovered moving his body eased tension built up during the meeting. He scanned the room as he set the final folding chair on the storage cart. The visitor, Ed, was gone. Stress escaped from his fingers.

****

Maylee pulled her rental car into the far right parking spot outside a popular convenience store. She flipped down the vanity mirror and fluffed her hair while watching Larry pump gas. Three blocks ago she'd picked up his trail from another detective. Her assignment was to follow him these final two miles and confirm when he entered his house.

A moment later she jotted a few words into her notebook, including the time Larry entered the store. Bright advertisements on the window blocked his movements inside the building, but she glimpsed him while he stood at the cashier. She started the engine and recorded the minute when he exited carrying a plastic bag.

She tailed him light, allowing up to three cars between them on the busiest street. When he turned the final corner, her task increased in difficulty. Not another vehicle moved for two blocks. She hesitated at the corner for a long moment and then drove slow and steady, as if looking for an address. Twice more she drove around a square route before calling Tom. "He's inside. One light at the side rear. Truck in the drive."

"Go home, Morgan. Patrol will sweep past every two hours."

"One more thing. I'll talk to the clerk while his memory's fresh." She ended the call and looked down the residential street. Thompson's truck appeared as a dark shadow sitting three lots from the corner. Across the narrow street, the porch light glowed on Mr.

Mueller's home. Was the neighbor watching? Would he call her in as a suspicious vehicle?

Fifteen minutes later, her interview with the clerk complete and the summary sent off to the case file notes, she drove toward Leine Street and home. A moment after the turn off Jefferson, her stomach rumbled and reminded her supper was late. She did a mental inventory of her fridge and placated her appetite with a promise of a portion of her mother's excellent meatloaf, reheated. *Hope the salad mix is still green and good.*

"What?" The empty air in Maylee's car didn't offer an explanation for the boxy red and white ambulance parked in front of her building with all its lights flashing.

After she parked her car in the lot beside Dave's compact orange hybrid, she entered the building. The back door, with plywood replacing the fractured glass, whispered shut behind her. Voices, more than one, all male, rose from the basement stairwell.

She advanced four steps before she recognized Dave's voice over the clutter. "No argument, Mrs. Gossen. You're going to the hospital."

"What happened?" She aimed her voice down the steps.

"Maylee?" Dave spoke over a softer conversation.

She wrapped one hand around the narrow rail mounted on the wall. "Yes."

"Join us. Watch your step, bulb in the hall is out down here." He cautioned.

"Be right back." Maylee turned and hurried away. The penlight on her person wouldn't add much, but the heavy duty portable in her kitchen would be stronger than the regular compact fluorescent in the ceiling fixture.

In record time she returned, stood beside a medical technician, and positioned her big, square flashlight. "Let them take care of you, Mrs. Gossen."

"Missed the last step. Never expected. Been down here half a dozen times today. The bulb burned out. It's been out all day. Know these steps like my own bedroom." The elderly lady rambled with only half her usual volume. "I'm not an invalid. Just help me up. I can wrap it good. I've got an almost new elastic bandage upstairs."

"Your leg needs an x-ray." Dave's tone didn't allow argument. "These abrasions on your arms and elbows deserve a proper cleaning. Maybe a stitch or two."

"But…but…"

"One ambulance ride, coming up." The tech stood, accepted one end of a back board from his partner, and motioned Maylee to step back.

"Where are you taking her? We should call her daughter."

"Grand Avenue Hospital is closest. Any objections, ma'am?" The tech slid a thin plastic splint under one ankle.

Maylee slipped into the tone of voice expected to receive the best results from nervous crime or accident witnesses. "I'll need your daughter's number. Where can I find it?"

"Adele. Call Adele. She lives close. Got her number here." Mrs. Gossen started to lift an arm, pointed her index finger toward her head, and groaned.

Maylee lifted her gaze from her phone in time to

see Dave waltz his fingers down Mrs. Gossen's raised arm. The man's hands exemplified grace and beauty. His fingertips moved along the elderly, fragile surface without a trace. The skin on Maylee's arms danced at the idea of his fingers caressing, soothing. She swallowed and stared.

"Easy now. Calm and still are your friends. Breathe light, like watching TV instead of running for the bus."

"You're making too much of this, Doc."

Maylee kept her disagreement silent. A person didn't need to be a medical expert to realize the elderly lady's foot lay at an unnatural angle. Distraction might be her neighbor's friend. "Do you remember the number? For Adele."

"Careful young man, my ankle hurts." Mrs. Gossen snapped as the backboard touched her leg. Then she took one quick, light breath and rattled off a number.

Maylee tapped it into her phone and stepped into the laundry room. Suddenly, the three bars on her phone display jumped to four. She found a place under the high window and waited during the phone's soft beeps of making a call. Multicolored ambulance lights pulsed into the room in a separate rhythm. Dave's arm bobbed in and out of sight through the open entrance. His voice drifted in soft and confident, untying the tight nerves under her ribs as she waited for an answer to her call.

"This is Adele Johnson. Who's calling?"

Mildred moaned, and the men exchanged quiet remarks. Maylee discarded the script she'd prepared. "I'm a friend and neighbor of Mildred Gossen."

"Granny? Has something happened?"

"I'm afraid so. Are you in a good place to talk?"

She drew a deep breath and gave the young woman at the other end of the connection an opportunity to do the same. Then she recited a brief description of a fall and transport by ambulance to Grand Avenue Hospital. "She's conscious, lucid, gave me your number right off."

"Have they gone? Can I have a word with her?"

Maylee attempted to picture Adele, one of three granddaughters who visited the building at irregular intervals. "They're outside, ready to leave. It's too late to hand her the phone."

"Okay. I'll get to the ER pronto." Adele spoke to another person too low for Maylee to decipher. "Thanks. I'll call Mother and the others."

Maylee disconnected the call and leaned against the plain table under the window. Options scrolled like a list.

Retreat to her apartment, her duty done.

Wait for Dave on the chance he would answer her questions.

Check the dryers for Mildred's clothes and fold them properly.

She stayed glued to the spot and studied the toes of her practical black shoes. The soft sound of one set of footsteps reached her over quiet thoughts. Slap, tap, hard shoes against the smooth tile in the hall announced Dave's arrival.

"Our patient missed more than one step."

She snapped her head up, alert at the unexpected statement. *Our patient?* "Did she lie there long?"

"No. I heard her fall. Or rather, her first outcry when she tumbled."

"She's lucky then. Regarding timeline." Maylee

slammed a mental door against memories of mixed results during her patrol years when performing requested welfare checks. Too many times they'd found injured people only after multiple hours, or in one case, more than a day. She took two steps and opened the first dryer. Her body insisted on movement while he stood in the center of the room, watching her, and taking up all the emotional space.

He cleared his throat, either unaware or ignoring the fact, he already held her full attention. "About yesterday. In the hospital room."

"We should have waited in the hall until you finished." She pulled a mound of cool clothes into her arms and transferred them to the table. If she kept her hands busy she might win the fight with temptation to put them where they didn't belong—against his arms or chest.

"I gave you permission without knowing who knocked." He pulled a washcloth from the jumbled garments and folded it into quarters. "Was he able to answer your questions? Solve the case from his sickbed?"

"He added information. Helpful." She forced her gaze away from his capable fingers.

"But he didn't name Dr. Saterro's murderer for you."

She shook a pair of practical underpants and began folding them. "No arrest." She glanced up and matched his serious expression. "Not every case has a smoking gun."

He stilled. She watched his face drain of color until it matched the worn white towel in his hand.

"It's a figure of speech. Dave?"

He swallowed, breathed, and showed signs of recovery. "Of course."

"Where do you go when you fade to match egg shells?"

"You don't need to know." He turned his attention to the fabric in his hands, folded it twice and reached for another. "It's not a happy place."

"Suspected as much." She shrugged as if to ignore him, but each time she reached for a sock to match in front of her, she stole a glance at his face. Did the past claim him with particular cues? *Not happy*. She did a mental match with the three times he'd reacted by a stumble back into this unhappy place of his. Nothing obvious in his background check indicated irrational fears of funerals or firearms. Listing an uncle as emergency contact made sense once we discovered his mother was in prison for years. His father's death? She crossed it off as an unlikely strong influence after two decades.

"I don't like guns. Smoking or any other kind."

If she'd not been listening, she'd have passed the sound off as a mumble. "Because…"

He tossed down the kitchen towel in his hand, marched away and turned at the doorway. "I've seen the holes they make in people."

****

"Coward." Dave threw the word against the kitchen cabinets as the door slammed behind him. "Giving half truths to her." He swung one leg over the faded vinyl of a kitchen chair and stacked his arms on the narrow back.

Apprehension, his little beast within, paced in a circle.

He didn't want to care. From the moment in the clinic when he'd learned her occupation, he wanted to avoid, ignore, and forget her. Instead, she poked into his life. She turned on a smile capable of warming him from the toes up when they crossed paths. She carried the scent of tropical flowers in small spaces. Decorated her ears with tiny pearls, the gem which he admired more than cut stones.

He closed his eyes for a moment and pictured her chatting with guests at the funeral visitation. She wore a skirt. And sheer black hose over perfect legs. She smiled small while talking and nodding to others.

And during the storm. He rested his chin on his arms and stared straight ahead. Warm rain, wool, and jungle flower scent in her hair. He couldn't resist. Mere flesh didn't stand a chance when she toppled into his arms. Instinct overwhelmed him, permitted, no—encouraged—the soft kiss behind her ear. He could feel her on his lips now, again, washed by nature. His body warmed, poked long suppressed hormones awake at the memory.

She's dangerous. Fear, or one of its close relatives, skipped across his shoulders. He needed to stop living this way. He would soon be out of places to run.

Classmates talked of deer hunting. He edged out of the circle.

A roommate sought out the army recruiter. He avoided meeting the soldier.

An armed patrol arrived at the mission clinic. He tended the wounded. During a break in his medical duties, he'd stood in the narrow doorway and used bad Spanish to order the rifles to stay outside the wards.

A neighbor needed transportation. A detective and

her gun rode beside him, sat across the table, selected new running shoes while he observed from a few feet away.

Maybe there's hope.

He turned on the heat under the teakettle and opened his door a few inches. She needed to pass this way. This set of stairs remained the logical route to her apartment regardless of the abrupt end to their conversation.

Five minutes later he listened as Mrs. Gossen's door opened and used it as a cue to step into the hall.

"Putting these inside." Maylee pointed to the stack of clothes she carried.

"Good." He nodded. Self-disappointment clogged his throat. It was time, past time, to put clumsy coping methods away. "I've got fresh cookies to talk over."

"I thought I caught a whiff of a bakery." She flashed a smile rousing Apprehension to watchfulness. A moment later she disappeared into the neighbor's apartment.

Dave waited, counted to five, then more seconds until she stepped into the hall, pulled the door tight, and tested the spring lock. He focused on her face, a view almost as beautiful as her legs. No, her feminine features, framed by short, soft brown hair held his attention better. Hints of confidence and intelligence escaped from her eyes and mouth to the world. He gestured to the carpeted stairs. "We could picnic on the steps."

She raised both brows and angled her head.

"House…rules," he stammered. "No guns allowed."

"No exceptions."

173

He blinked, searching for the confidence of a minute ago. "None whatsoever."

"I admire your principles."

It's more a survival tactic. He moved his gaze over her, admiring her textbook posture and the hint of ladylike curves under clothing more than invisible principles.

"Will you take a rain check?"

He crossed his arms and rested one shoulder on the wall. "I'll pray for rain."

She stepped past him to the stairs and laughed.

The sound bounced off the bare walls, lingering an instant after she moved out of sight. He retreated to his apartment. *Go to sleep.* He gave a silent command to Apprehension and turned off the stove.

He'd take a vivid memory of Maylee's smile and laughter to bed with him.

Chapter Fourteen

Seen the holes they make. No exceptions. Maylee shook her head, but Dave's words continued to circle. They'd invaded the ritual cleaning of Angel, her Glock 19, late last night. This morning they accompanied the motion of settling the holster on her hip. Part of her wanted to dismiss them as related to a hectic shift in the emergency department. Yet…the tone was more personal.

She opened the next folder on the stack and set a letter beside three others on the table. When her brain didn't recycle his words, it played with his image. Her sleep last night included recurring memories of strong, trained fingers on fragile skin. At dawn, the memory of the scent around him in the laundry room, butter, sugar, and warm vanilla, returned. In the next breath she detected a whiff of something stronger, more associated with morning.

"Greetings, Morgan." Ed Jamison set a large paper cup of coffee on the table. "French roast, black. Word is you like your brew strong and dark."

"Correct." She smiled, lifted the cup, and inhaled one of her favorite aromas. "Did the AA meeting go well?"

He shrugged, turned a chair around, and straddled it. "Full report is in the book."

She nodded. Five minutes ago she'd printed out her

own report of last night's observation of Lawrence Thompson and added it to the Saterro case master file.

"Starting the party without me?" Tom saluted them with a cup from his favorite fast food place. "What should I know?"

Jamison cleared his throat. "Thompson either suspected I was a plant or is naturally cautious. A good part of the time he behaved distracted, as if thinking about something not related to the meeting. His girlfriend, on the other hand, wanted to carry on conversations with everyone in the room."

Maylee nodded and focused her memory on the only time she'd encountered Larry Thompson and Sandra Holmes together. She'd been the more outgoing of the two during quick introductions in the parking lot. Of course, Larry recognized her from their official visit the previous day. Quiet and cautious could be his nature. "Was he possessive?"

"Of her? Yeah. She didn't push back enough for most people to notice. I don't trust him." Jamison concluded.

"Neither do we." Tom gulped the last of his coffee. "We're pursuing enough evidence to get a search warrant for his truck and home. That's why I sent you to the meeting. Any hint of violence in our man?"

"Not when I stood within hearing distance. He didn't talk much. Looked preoccupied. Hedged on giving a sobriety date." Jamison stood as his phone buzzed. "They want me downstairs. My gut feeling is Thompson's going to get tripped up in his lies soon. But I didn't get you any closer to a warrant."

"No further away, either. Until next time?" Tom waved the patrol corporal on his way.

Maylee set down her coffee. "Thompson made a stop between dropping off his date and getting home."

"So you mentioned in your call."

"I swung back and checked with the clerk. He wasn't certain, but the register tape showed a cash sale for two packs of cigarettes and a bottle of Tennessee whiskey at the right time."

Tom sighed and offered her a mint. "He might be tempting himself. Changing habits can involve rituals, many of which appear odd to others. I kept a pack of smokes in the glove box for six months. Guess I wanted to prove I could resist."

"Did you?"

He looked up at the ceiling longer than a lighting inspector before mixing words in a noisy exhale. "Few close calls. But back to Thompson. Patrol recorded his truck at the warehouse this morning, so I doubt he's cracked the seal on any alcohol."

"Good." She turned to the letters spread out on the table. "It gives us more time to find an author for these. I've color coded several key words: justice, innocent, truth, and favored."

"Did you include your letters?"

She held her breath, a reflex at mention of the messages addressed to her. The second anonymous threat arrived Friday, but with the storm and the resulting damage, it was Saturday morning before she checked her mailbox. "Yes. Both."

"Bad signature." He pointed to the first letter to the prosecuting attorney's office, the only one with a hint of authorship. "My doc scribbles better."

"General consensus of officers on the case goes with the letter near the middle as a 'T.' Do you think a medical person would have better luck?" She pressed her lips tight and felt her neck warm. The first medical person who came to mind was Dave. And she could imagine him looking at the scrawl, gifting a smile, and going silent.

"Comparison?"

"Screen on your left." She pointed to a display of Larry Thompson's and Tony Lorenti's driver's licenses. "These are recent, twelve years after the letter. Signatures change. At least, I know mine has since high school."

"For the better?"

"You wish." She tapped her pencil against the orange highlighted word, justice, and counted in a whisper. On the third occurrence she stalled, read the complete sentence twice. "What do you think of this?"

"She rests uneasy, waiting for the scales of justice to balance."

Tom glanced to the next sheet of paper, dated a month later. "Not enough for a warrant. Even if we could get all the arrows to point to Thompson at the same time, it remains conjecture."

"So we wait for him to get drunk and explode?"

"Not exactly. We increase patrols past his house. Where does his girlfriend work?"

She typed the name Sandra Holmes and added "cosmetologist" as a search word. "Yes, the woman is related to my neighbor. His mother. Convicted felon released on parole seven years ago. I've not explored the details of her case."

"Maybe it's time we explored the Holmes family." Tom grabbed the mouse on the second computer.

Maylee blocked out his off tune wordless rendition

of a Beatles song. It resembled "Yellow Submarine," but with her partner's lack of musical ability, it could be another one. "Found her." She jotted down the name and address of Sandra's current employer. "She's met me. Would it be better if you got the haircut?"

"Don't think we need to become customers." He turned the monitor to give her a better view.

Maylee glanced at Sandra's demographic information before reading the case summary and focusing in on a crime scene photo. A man lay in an undisturbed pool of his own blood. The simple caption, "S. Holmes" with the date and location, clarified Dave's house rule against guns.

****

Larry advanced into the small office and stopped one military pace from the table. He glanced at the two small stacks of brown envelopes and gulped. Reflexes and nerves held taut for the entire morning threatened to empty breakfast out of his stomach. The previous time he'd been the helpless supplicant was years ago, when Barbara's family ignored him. He struggled to put a good face on this employment decision today and get it over with. "Thompson, Lawrence J."

"I'm sorry, Mr. Thompson."

I'm out then. He swallowed hard and focused on the younger man, the same corporation suit which interviewed him yesterday.

"Several of the other warehouse workers have more experience and seniority. You'll be paid for all your unused vacation days plus the"—he checked a chart—"ten days termination and sick leave pay. This will be direct deposit, a separate transaction from wages earned this week. Questions?"

179

Larry rubbed one thumb against fingers pleading to curl into a fist. Weeks of rumors and worse case scenarios crashed over him. His nightmare unrolled in a tiny office scented with clean cardboard and spicy after-shave. "So I'm done when I walk out of here?" He waited for the younger man to nod before he picked up the envelope with his name in the corner. "Papers inside repeat what you said? Get me started at the unemployment office?"

"You'll be getting a good reference, Mr. Thompson."

Larry studied the man across the table. Neither worry nor smile lines had found time to etch themselves on the face. Larry released a soft snort. "Whole lot needs to happen before I ask for a reference. You, your company, entire group of you, are not my friends." He turned, took a step, pivoted back. "I'll be going now. I know my way to my truck."

"Good luck, Mr. Thompson." The other man stood and extended his hand.

With a shake of his head, Larry spun away and strode out the door. He'd take his pride home with him. He wouldn't let an out-of-state kid still learning to shave think a handshake erased corporate actions.

Half an hour later, Larry stood in the open toolshed door and lit a cigarette. One of the sudden, intense showers common during Midwest springs splashed down two steps away. He blew out words with the first stream of smoke. "So much for yard work. Need to keep my hands busy."

He closed his eyes and ran a couple experimental sentences through his mind. He didn't want to tell Sandra he'd lost his job. He didn't want to tell his sister, Betty, either.

Betty and her husband read the newspaper, almost every word. Did the sale of Yates Distributing show up on the business page? Would he face a barrage of questions and suggestions when he went over on Sunday?

He shook his head and stared at the toes of his work boots. How long could he delay telling either woman? Could he lie by omission until he found a job? New job could be months away. A man at the end of the block, a machinist, limped along with odd jobs after a year.

"Don't have money for long." He tallied up unemployment benefits and the modest number in his bank account. If his truck held up, and the roof didn't start to leak, he could manage—until tax time at the end of the year.

He needed reassurance, a sensible person to talk with. Another strong pull on the smoke cleared fog out of his brain. He pulled out his phone and hit the single button to call Sandra.

"Hi. This is a surprise." She picked up an instant before it went to voice mail. "Are you calling from work?"

"Got off early. Work's crazy and confused. I'll tell you about it when it settles again." He spaced the lies by forming pictures of her in one of the bright floral print tops she favored at work. He liked her blue ones. They seemed to bring out her blue eyes.

"Then say your piece. We're swamped. Lori called in, and we're each taking a portion of her clients."

He tapped off ash and hunted for words. "Can we get together tonight? Collect the rain check on your brownies?"

"Too late. Brought them to work today and they vanished. And tonight's not good for me. I'm here until closing. Then I'll be falling asleep in front of the Cardinals game."

"Tomorrow then. A nice long talk after our meeting."

"Sounds good. Oh, got to run. Timer went off for a perm."

"Take care, Sandra. I…" He sighed as the click of her disconnect reached his ear. He may as well go in the house and poke around on his computer. He could check an employment site or two before fixing supper.

He entered the kitchen and gazed at the bottle on the table. The container was squared off, the perfect size for his hand to lift. The amber liquid whispered an invitation. He studied the seal on the neck for a long moment and took one step forward. He reached out and ran his index finger along the label's edge. A shot would feel good about now. Nice counter-action to the chill from the rain.

A moment later he found a shot glass, broke the seal, and poured. "Medicinal purposes."

Familiar heat filled his throat. An old friend welcomed back after a long absence.

"Need to be careful." He skimmed one hand over the familiar shape of the glass neck. The bottle and the golden brown liquid it held were beautiful things. The whiskey sparkled in the overhead light, pretty enough to lead him into trouble. He smiled as the memories of several such occasions spun through his mind. "Whiskey and women. So much joy." He set the glass beside the bottle and turned away. "Joy followed by misery. I need to be careful."

He filled the next three hours with browsing the employment web sites, doing a load of laundry, and tidying the kitchen. After each household task or completed job application he drank another shot as his reward. The first third of the bottle vanished. The computer directions became a little harder to follow. He fixed a fried egg sandwich when his stomach growled in hunger, took his evening medicines all at once, and washed them down with his liquid friend.

After his meal, he settled in his worn leather recliner, half a tumbler of whiskey in one hand and the TV remote in the other. *I'll pretend tomorrow is Saturday. Heck, I've a whole string of Saturdays now.* The show got a little fuzzy. He closed his eyes, intending to rest them for a minute.

Larry jerked awake, raised his hand to rub his eyes, and listened. His phone over on the table slipped into voice mail.

"Hi, sweetie. It's me. Called to let you know I'm home. Expect I'll be asleep before the Cardinals break the tie. No need to call back. We'll talk tomorrow."

He levered up out of the chair and stared down at the phone. He jabbed a button and the message repeated. "Sweetie. Barbara uses the same word." He shook his head, regretted the motion as his world tilted. For a moment, he stiffened his arm on the table for support. Yep, his old buddy from Tennessee went down smooth and sneaked up later swinging a big bat. He gathered a fresh lungful of air, walked over to the calendar, and stared at the month and year in large letters for a long moment. "Barbara's dead. Murdered by a careless doctor. No justice from the law."

Barbara. My true love. Larry braced one hand on the wall and allowed his mind to drift back in time. The hospital staff and her parents turned him into a beggar for a rushed farewell. He glanced down at his hand; the same hand caressed her swollen face all those years ago. Fluids dripped into tubes in her arms, and a machine hissed as it mimicked breathing. "I promised you justice. I'm sorry you've waited so long."

He turned back to the table, grazed his fingertips across the tops of the prescription bottles, and lifted the short, squat one. Blinking the print into focus he read aloud. "One in the evening, for sleep. Do not drive for seven hours." A moment later he swallowed a capsule, grasped the bottle, and stared at the final inch of temptation. He raised it to his lips. "No reason to pretend. Anymore."

Chapter Fifteen

"Brainless wonder." Maylee flicked a cardboard beer coaster toward the young man across the tall round table. Her words dissolved in noisy confusion. The Rolling Stones blared from the speakers and Cardinal baseball highlights flashed on huge screens. The popular downtown sports bar bubbled with laughter and conversation of fans after a win.

"You'll hurt my feeiings."

"Single." She held up one finger. "If you've even one left."

"Give him a break," Kate urged. "Brian reverts to the manners and intellect of a first grader after three beers. I pity his future wife."

"It could be you." Brian lifted Kate's arm and placed a sloppy kiss on the inside of her elbow.

"Ehhhew." She jerked her arm away and reached for a crumpled napkin. "After the Cubs win the World Series…three times…in a row."

"Geeze. You girls are rough."

"High standards. You should try it sometime." Kate laughed.

Maylee glanced at her companions. It raised her spirits to see her friend smile and joke again. Since her uncle's death, Kate appeared either subdued in her own grief or exhausted from playing nice with relatives. Tonight, until after the game, she'd been evasive—or at least reluctant—each time Maylee inquired about the electronic pen pal.

Brian's friends shook their heads and muttered their pity.

"And the hour is late, getting later." Maylee shoved money for her lemonade and appetizer under one of the glasses littered across the table. The original post game plan consisted of one quick drink here while traffic cleared out. But plans go astray. First, it had taken the Cardinals twelve innings to win. Then, while exiting the stadium, a trio of Kate's high school friends happened along. Almost two hours of eating, drinking, and laughing later, she checked her pockets and belt before leaving the table.

"Leaving so soon?" Brian signaled a server.

"Work later this morning." Maylee paused with her hand on his shoulder and spoke to the server. "Coffee for him. And no car keys."

"Says who?"

Maylee made eye contact with the most sober of Brian's friends. "Will you see him home?"

"Yes, ma'am. Nice police officer, ma'am." The blond with a mustache lifted an empty soda glass in salute and promise.

She returned a crisp two-finger salute. *Ethan. Never gave a last name.* She tucked his name away for use in future conversations.

Kate completed her departing bows and led them toward the exit.

Wow. It felt good to laugh. Not the tight, controlled snicker or polite chuckle she responded with around her co-workers, but real, no-volume-control bursts. "Where have you been hiding those guys?"

"Deep in the rock garden." Kate eased into step beside her. "Would you believe they've improved since high school?"

"Anything you say." Maylee turned toward the stadium garage and adjusted her stride to match Kate's shorter stature. What would it be like to make this walk with Dave? Attend a game with him? Share laughs? Had she ever heard him utter anything on the relaxed side of neutral?

Once upon a time, she scrolled her thoughts back to the only near normal conversation between them. A discussion of dogs and brothers filled the walk home from the park. What day did the run and encounter with a family in crisis at the dog park occur? A week ago? No. A few days more. A week ago Monday. The same day the video techs removed Dave from the suspect list.

Dinner after an arrest. She crossed her fingers, wished for a warrant. This case invaded too many portions of her life. Until tonight—the first activity without threads back to neighbors, suspects, and anonymous threats.

"Is your family going to the Saturday Cardinals game Memorial Day weekend this year?" Kate asked.

"Absolutely." Maylee glanced at her friend. She needed a date for the game. Ethan, the sober one from tonight? She could ask Kate for an email address. No, she'd want an explanation.

"Is your new neighbor going?"

She skipped a step, recovered, and glanced at Kate. "I've not asked." The case, with the names of his mother and her friend still embedded in the investigation, descended over her mood like a black blanket. "He lives downstairs. End of story."

"Really?" Kate stopped and began ticking snatches of between-inning conversations off like baseball statistics. "Surgeon at Grand Avenue Hospital. Jogs at Saxon Park. Likes dogs. Cooks. Drives a Prius. Doesn't sound like the end of any story I know."

Maylee continued to move her gaze in a pattern and led them into the stadium garage. *Ask Dave. Need an arrest first.* "My rental's on third. I'll give you a ride to your car."

****

Larry drove past the building, circled around, and passed it again before he parked his truck at the end of the block. For a long moment he stared at the streetlamps standing in an even row and the additional light over the door. *Tonight. Justice is within sight.* He reached into the glove box and tucked his late father's snub-nosed revolver into his belt.

"A good soldier prepares for the mission." Larry touched the hilt of his favorite Bowie knife with his left thumb as he marched toward the private parking lot. He thanked the army for combat drills. During advanced training he'd been good with a knife. And he still knew how to travel quiet, stay in the shadows, and wait.

He stepped around the end of a short, solid fence hiding large garbage and recycle bins. Her car was missing. Good. He stood stiff, his eyes the only body part in motion, quiet as a sentry on duty. Small security lights at the high corners of the building cast light while leaving narrow bands of deep shadow. *Good night for outdoor work.*

A battle waged within his body. His liver, damaged by heavy drinking for decades, struggled to metabolize the fifth of whiskey, sparse supper, and seven different medications carried in his blood. Alcohol alone, any one of the prescription drugs, or his over-the-counter allergy pills in isolation, would have posed a difficult task for his damaged liver. He stood still, uninterested in the interior struggle going on at a molecular level. It was slow work for an abused organ to break the multitude of chemicals into pieces. At the moment his internal switchboard flickered, overloaded with requests.

The antihistamine jostled with the sedative. Molecules of the calcium blocker insisted on being processed before the antidepressant. Chemical chains of statin wrapped around portions of the atypical antipsychotic compound queued behind alcohol. His light supper supplied albumin and gluten. Blood carried more and more unprocessed chemicals to his brain where they confused delicate neurons and blocked key pathways.

Larry drifted up and down the awareness scale, from totally alert and waiting, to dim knowledge of standing outside. He memorized the license plate on the small car next to the empty space. *Assigned parking.* He scrolled one version of the near future through his mind. He'd move fast, before his target found an opportunity to sound an alarm.

"Tonight I get justice. I'm doing this for you, Barbara." He closed his eyes for a long moment and imagined his best girl on her best day. He pictured her oval face—how a gentle smile and laughter in her eyes reminded him of an angel after he told an old army story cleaned up for her delicate ears.

Another memory, this one from her funeral, bubbled up and took over his thoughts. Her parents, aunts, uncles, cousins, and strangers to him filled the front pews of Our Lady of Sorrows. He tugged on the sleeve of his only suit, a dark brown in a sea of black. Through unblotted tears he tallied the flower arrangements, counted them twice to confirm the special pink roses he'd paid for, were missing. Heat swelled deep in his gut, looking for an escape.

Light washed over him, bringing him back to a May night. He froze in anticipation as a car arrived and turned into the parking space.

He pulled in a deep breath, nodded to the invisible Barbara beside him, and stepped forward. Plans for a quick intercepting dash changed when his right foot dragged on the asphalt. He used precious breath on a string of soft swear words.

A moment later Larry straightened in a sliver of deep shadow. He called up a reserve of air and shouted to the figure emerging from the car. "You. Now. It's over."

****

"How old are your shoes, Sandra." Dave sat on the edge of his bed and scrubbed one hand across his face. Between his fingers he made out the time on the clock. Past one in the morning, and Sandra had chattered on for five minutes already.

"It's my back, David. Not an ache in my feet keeping me awake."

"Yes. I know. You said back." *Three times.* "Have you taken any painkillers?"

"Of course. During the ninth inning. When I thought the game would end soon and I'd be getting to bed at a reasonable hour."

He turned the phone away from his mouth before

he sighed. Sandra experienced the results of addiction. She faced her own alcohol-specific brand and remained terrified of either prescription or over-the-counter drug dependency. She preferred talk therapy. With family. At any hour.

"Are you listening, David?"

"I'm thinking." He stood and gave a brief, longing glance at his pillow. "If I give you a suggestion will you hang up and follow it?"

"It's too soon for any more medicine."

"I'm advising music. Put on the 'Sounds of the Seashore' or whatever the title on the CD Joe gave you. Add a cup of hot, herbal tea for good measure."

"That's all?"

"I still suspect your shoes." He took a few steps and stretched. A few more minutes of this, and he'd need to follow his own advice.

Sandra replied with a combination snort and laugh. "A man's telling me to go shopping. The world must be near its end."

"And if it happens before dawn you've even saved shoe money. I'm gone." Dave ended the call before Sandra could speak. *Since I'm out of bed.* He walked into the main room and hesitated in front of the dining area window. A moment later, he spread two slats and peered out. Maylee's parking space remained empty. Exactly the same as it had since he'd come home from work.

Was she working? Following a suspect on the city streets? He closed his eyes to imagine her profile. For an instant his mind formed a perfect picture of her studying papers on a table, writing notes in a blend of cursive and printing. *Arrest him.*

"And then what?" he asked the empty room. He had eleven months and two weeks of lease remaining as her neighbor. It would be impossible to avoid her. Did he want to? Maylee the person tugged, invited him to come close. Last night, he'd been intoxicated with her calm efficiency obtaining the necessary phone number. He couldn't believe the events in the laundry room were only a day ago. They almost touched elbows folding clothes. He shook his head at memory of his invitation for cookies and tea on the steps.

"One item." He sighed. Maylee the neighbor, the running partner, the dinner companion pulled him back for more. The other thing—the gun—what name did she call it? Angel? It was black like the devil.

He replayed their single conversation about firearms. He'd started it, while waiting for dinner after the storm.

"Are you always armed?"

"Absolutely. Right arm." She thrust it out straight. *"Left arm is mirror image but needs a little extra attention to maintain equal strength and agility. And Angel. Don't worry about her. She's shy and minds her manners."*

"Angel?"

She tapped her holster through her jacket. *"My Guardian Angel. Glock 19. Dependable. Everything a service weapon should be. Stays right on my hip everywhere I go."*

Dave startled as his phone announced an incoming text. He glanced down and smiled as he read Sandra's complaint about the suggested music.

"House rule. No firearms." He whispered his own commandment; the one which trembled violently when the polite, neighborly thing would have been to invite Maylee across the threshold last night. In the end, she'd declined his compromise of a picnic on the steps. Perhaps it was for the best. Explanations of the sort she deserved would go better in a different setting.

Light washed over the window beside him. He peeked between the slats and confirmed it was Maylee's car coming to rest beside his Prius. Out of habit, he scanned as much of the lot as he could see in the almost overlapping pools of light.

Did something move? Near the dumpster?

Chapter Sixteen

Maylee cupped the keys in her left hand and closed the car door.

"It's over."

Her senses went on alert while her mind repeated the unexpected words. *It's over. What's over?*

She turned toward the male voice and scanned deep into the shadows. Three normal steps and she stood at the rear bumper. Cones of light from the street and the security lights on the building touched without overlapping on the asphalt. The only space large enough to hide a human was a narrow path of shadow leading out from the dumpster and its short fence. "Tell me more. Explain it."

A dark clad figure moved at the rim of the streetlight's reach. "Justice."

She cataloged the hoarse voice, size, and posture to determine a middle-aged male confronted her. He spoke slow, as if probing for and examining each word before releasing it toward her. Drunk? High on drugs?

She steadied her gaze on him and favored the first. A majority of the street drugs made their victims fast-talking, nervous, and prone to random movement. Alcohol, on the other hand, slowed reflexes.

A baseball cap shielded his face, making it difficult to tie his features to a name. She began to ease forward, attempting to move him toward the cone of the security light. "I need more information. Justice is a big topic."

She moved two fingers on her right hand until they touched the base of Angel's holster. Security, backup, tool of last resort—the department nicknames flashed for an instant of comfort. "Who are you?"

"I'm…not…important.   I…don't…matter."   He shuffled back and to the side, keeping his feet in shadow while his profile edged closer to a beam of light.

"Wrong." She used the command tone most apt to make suspects and dogs pay attention. "Who needs this justice? Why do you think I hold it?"

"Don't…" His voice got lost in the space between them.

She advanced two small, slow steps away from the Prius' rear fender. Her right hand clenched and released, preparing, staying ready for a quick grab. She'd go for Angel only if necessary. She drew a cautious breath, blew it out mixed with frustration when she realized her phone rested in her right coat pocket— Impossible to reach while staying weapon ready. "Why me? What brings you here for justice?"

"Stay put."

What's he carrying? She leaned back an inch without moving her feet and focused on his hands. It took a moment to realize he wore tight, dark gloves. She flicked her gaze upward as he moved enough for a portion of his face to be displayed in the security light. *Thompson?* Her chest froze until he nodded at her silent recognition. She slid her left foot forward.

He moved his left hand and a knife blade flashed in the pale light. "Halt."

"Put the weapon down, Thompson. Talk this out.

Your combat knife will do nothing but put you in worse trouble."

"Don't think so." He backed another step and rotated his wrist. The security light above the door bathed his side, throwing his shadow to his feet. "You…your father…as good as killed her."

"Barbara?"

"Who else matters? Not me. You…they…all of them…proved it."

"It was an accident." She reviewed the information from the official reports and the interview with Mr. Trudeau at lightning speed. Barbara Trudeau didn't plan to marry Thompson. All the parties involved except Thompson understood she disliked his drinking. "Barbara's death was tragic."

He stilled the knife before standing for a moment at attention. Then he raised his voice into the mild, spring air. "Crime. Murdered. By the high and mighty doctor."

"What are you looking for?" She alternated her gaze by fractions of a second between his face and the knife blade. Lessons from the academy surged forward in her mind. Adrenaline rushed to her fingertips and she slowed it with a measured breath. *Keep him talking. Don't get either of us hurt.*

"Justice." His right hand darted toward his belt.

Maylee pulled Angel out of her holster and extended her right arm. In the same instant she squeezed the key fob, setting off the lights and horn on her rental car. She brought her left arm up to brace her weapon, allowing the keys to plop at her feet. "Drop the knife. And the gun."

Larry's eyes widened and his mouth pursed as he clutched the knife and pointed a revolver. "No."

She gazed at his face for one second before settling her stare on his hands. A slight tremble of the blade demonstrated he held, but did not control the weapons. "Drop them."

"Make me."

****

Dave stood glued to the floor and stared between the slats. He drew a shallow breath and held it as a man took shape in the weak light outside. He couldn't hear any words passing between the intruder and Maylee, but he understood body language. She wanted the stranger to leave.

Who would be waiting in the dark? Could it be a homeless man off his psychiatric drugs? He blinked away the idea. In his limited encounters with individuals living on the streets, they acted non-confrontational. He could picture one scurrying off when discovered in the act of dumpster diving. This man moved with bravado.

A knife blade glinted when the man's arm moved.

Dave sucked in a breath and reached for his phone. It lay one step away, resting on the table with the text from Sandra displayed. He released the blinds, scooped up the device and dialed 911. "Send the police to 3200 Leine. In the Saxon neighborhood."

He returned to the window and pushed the blinds aside before the operator completed the next line on her script.

"What is your emergency?"

A stray syllable escaped. He swallowed quickly, forced his words to be clear and spaced. "Need police. He's got a knife. In the parking lot."

"Are you being threatened?"

"Not me. She. Detective Morgan. At 3200 Leine." All moisture fled from his mouth as Maylee moved forward, forcing the man back another step.

The operator's voice faded as Dave's thoughts spiraled back in time. Once again he became an eight-year-old boy waiting for the right moment to ask a question.

Sam Holmes sang the chorus of "The Gambler" as he came in the back door.

Dave peeked around the archway edge. His mother, Sandra, sat with her back to him. An empty gin bottle, glass, and full ashtray littered the table in front of her.

"You're late," she snapped at her husband. "Again."

"Stopped off with some of the guys. One beer. That's all."

"I want you gone. Now."

"It's late. I'm tired." He leaned against the end of the kitchen counter. "You're drunk. Let it wait until morning."

"No." She lifted grandpa's revolver from her lap and pointed it at Sam.

"Whoa." Sam raised his hands level with his shoulders and displayed his palms. "Put that thing away. Before somebody gets hurt."

"Go."

An explosion ripped the air.

Dave clamped both hands across his mouth and stared at his father.

Sam moved a hand to his neck where blood spurted through his fingers. He gave a slight nod before sliding to the floor.

Dave stood an instant longer watching a thread of smoke rise from the gun dropped on the table.

Beep. Beep. Amber and red lights flashed from a parked car outside the glass.

Dave managed a deep breath and pulled his mind back to the present. The operator asked another question but the words blurred in his head. "Can you repeat?"

"Sir. Units have been dispatched."

****

Maylee focused on Thompson's hands. She held Angel steady with both arms, sighted mere inches above the target's waist, and eased another small step forward. "Drop the weapons."

"Too late." The knife twitched as he backed half a step.

She moved her foot, confident Thompson would continue to move toward the building. Each movement brought a flash of memory. How many times had she pulled her service weapon on duty? Ten—in six years—every one stamped in living color in a section of brain marked "only with other law enforcement."

Drug dealers. Car thieves. Officers shoulder to shoulder, or at least within sight. Holding. Waiting. Flinching when the officer next to her fired into the nearest car. Her assigned vehicle.

No similarities with tonight surfaced as she stared at nervous hands encased in tight, dark gloves. "Drop them."

"Barbara. Doing this for Barbara. Can't you see?"

She focused on a dangerous, mentally disturbed drunk. "It was an accident. Drop the weapons. Then we can talk about Barbara."

"Fancy doctor murdered her." He shuffled back half a step.

"Accident. Tragic accident." She stared at his gun hand.

He stopped, lowered the knife until it paralleled his thigh. "Too late to talk. Lawyer…Morgan…didn't want to see it. Good as killed her again."

"Drop the weapons, Thompson."

He moved his foot back, contacted the concrete parking curb with his heel, and lost his balance. "No."

Maylee surged forward. She kicked his wrist to dislodge the gun as he went down on his back in the narrow space between parking block and building. An instant later she tossed the knife aside, rolled him to his stomach, and pulled one arm behind his back. She worked by memory, all the practice at the police academy keeping her hands and arms in rhythm as she applied the cuffs.

Approaching sirens registered as she paused for a breath. She kept her knee on his back and recited. "Lawrence Thompson, you are under arrest for assaulting a police officer. And other charges to follow. You have the right to remain silent…"

Lights from two police cruisers swept over the parking lot as they pulled in.

Maylee looked up, raised her badge in one hand to get attention. "Over here. One suspect. Disarmed."

****

"She didn't shoot." Dave blurted the words as he stepped through the door into the parking lot. He tried to ignore the first human blocking his way, pushed against a strong arm, and took another step toward Maylee. She stood in a small knot of people snug against the building surrounding a prone figure, the attacker.

"Step back, sir." Hard fingers tightened against his shoulder.

Dave blinked, halted, and faced the uniformed officer. Red, blue, and amber lights flashed and pulsed over the parking lot. Close to a dozen officers and first responders darted between a nearly equal number of vehicles. He licked his lips and forced words. "She…Detective Morgan…is she injured?"

"The situation is under control. Who are you? What did you see?"

"I…I…" He forced his gaze away from Maylee and her immediate companions and focused on the speaker. Blue shirt, rank stripes on the sleeve, and a name-tag declaring the name "Turner." "From my window," he pointed. "Saw her drive in—most of what followed. Called it in."

"We need to talk."

Dave sighed. An interview was inevitable. Yet—he stared at two officers guiding the suspect to his feet. A pulse of blue light illuminated Thompson's face, giving him a sickly skin. "Him? How? Why?"

"Your name?" Officer Turner claimed his attention.

"Holmes. David. Can we talk inside?"

The officer stayed silent for a long moment before exchanging hand signals with a co-worker. "You lead. I'll be one step behind."

Afraid I'll run? The way Dave assessed the current coordination in his legs, he'd collapse before making it to the building front entrance. He pushed through a group of fellow residents arrayed in nightwear before gesturing to his open apartment door. How long since he'd sprinted out, bare feet, no keys, and intent on seeing what happened after Maylee darted forward? Minutes? The numbers comprising hours and minutes tumbled in his mind.

"I…Can…Need a minute." Dave grabbed the first glass on the counter and began to fill it with cold water. Apprehension, his overactive companion, burst out of his trance and started a gymnastics routine within Dave's stomach. Dave opened a drawer, snatched a roll of antacids, and thumbed two into his palm.

"What did you see?" Officer Turner closed the door two-thirds before pulling out a small notebook.

Dave chewed antacid and added a gulp of water. His gaze found Officer Turner's weapon and stalled. *Gun in my house. Invited.* "From the window," Dave pointed. "Couldn't hear. I glimpsed a knife. He threatened my neighbor. I called."

A few minutes later, with colored lights continuing to sweep into the room, Dave glanced out the open blinds. Maylee stood beside a patrol car, talking on a phone, and gesturing with her free hand. She looked safe. Unharmed. *She didn't shoot.* "Detective Morgan lives upstairs."

"Did you recognize the suspect?"

Apprehension, his active beast within, paused his acrobatic routine. Dave could imagine the furry creature poised on hind legs, listening to the conversation. Silence within the room emphasized the lights still pulsing red and blue against pale walls. Each sip of water moistened his mouth for mere seconds before it again dried to the texture of sand.

"At the end." Dave faced his interviewer. "Not

until the officers walked him toward the cruiser."

"How do you know him?"

Good question. He stared at his phone resting on the table. For a moment he expected Sandra's voice to explode from it, demanding explanations he didn't have. "He's dating my mother. Sandra Holmes. I've seen him half a dozen times. Maybe less."

"Most recent time? Before tonight." Officer Turner stayed on topic.

Dave ran a quick review of this week. Sandra called multiple times a day. He'd spent a large portion of Sunday with her. When had Larry been there? Only the once at the apartment. "Sunday. A week ago. They—Larry and Sandra—brought dessert and looked at the apartment." *Turned pale as a corpse at the sight of Maylee.* "I headed out for hospital rounds after they left. Six? Quarter of?"

Several minutes and questions later, a tap on the partially open door was followed by Detective Tom Wilson. "Good. Exactly the men I wanted to see."

"Sir?" Officer Turner hurried to his feet.

"How far along are you?" Tom addressed the policeman.

"Almost done."

Dave glanced at Tom and words tumbled out. "Is she okay? Did he hurt her? Can I talk to her?"

"Whoa, Doc." Tom held up one palm. "Detective Morgan is in excellent health. Very busy. She will be for hours."

Dave fought off a memory of another detective, in another time and place, forbidding a request. *Never spoke to dad. Not the night it mattered.* Apprehension halted his sprint and somersaulted to a halt inside him.

"Are we done then?" He stared at Tom and counted. Five seconds. If they took their guns and left he might be able to breathe normal.

"I'll stay in touch." Tom gestured Officer Turner toward the door.

"One question, detective." Dave caught up to Tom before he crossed the threshold. "Why? What did Maylee...Detective Morgan...do to become a target?"

Chapter Seventeen

Dave reached for a towel to blot off water and a final speck of shaving cream. The early morning TV anchor began announcing the overnight arrests. He paused in the bathroom entrance and paid attention as the still photos of suspects for various crimes went on display next to the overly cheerful announcer.

Two arrested during an armed robbery in North County.

A parking lot brawl on the Illinois side of the river put three more into custody.

Larry's photo went up, and Dave lost track of the audio.

A moment later the screen changed to a scene of a fatal auto accident.

Dave released breath he'd held too long and turned away from the TV. He was still centering the towel on the rack when his phone rang. Within him, his furry beast, Apprehension, woke from a nap and began morning calisthenics. Only two places called at five in the morning—Sandra or the hospital. The safe bet at this moment would be Sandra.

"David, did you see the news? What happened? Can you help me arrange his bail?"

"Good Thursday morning to you too, Sandra."

"I'm serious, David. It has to be a mistake."

He poured toasted oat circles into a bowl and

settled into preparing his simple breakfast with one hand. "I watched the news. Bail isn't your responsibility."

"I have a little money set aside."

The line went quiet. Dave grasped the milk jug. "Sandra?"

"Still here. Lawrence has a sister. I'll look for her number. It's more logical for her to make bond arrangements."

"Slow down and let the system work." He poured milk and jabbed a clean spoon into the mound of cereal. He blinked away the image of Larry stumbling across the parking lot between a police officer and an EMT. He suspected the man belonged in a hospital bed, or at least a cot in a quiet room, while he recovered from his fall. But they'd taken him away in a police cruiser, not the ambulance.

"I need to find out where it happened. The news announcement only said the Saxon neighborhood. Did you hear a commotion? Was it near you? Were you—?"

He sank down on the nearest chair. Sandra's questions hit tender spots and disturbed closed mental doors. He focused on the slice of parking lot available from this angle. If he didn't move, he wouldn't see crime tape and yellow markers where the police gathered evidence last night. He expected them to return after sunrise for another round of photographs and searching. He swallowed twice and found a flat voice. "Larry attacked a police officer outside my window."

"I'm sorry, David." Sandra's voice reached him after a full minute delay.

It was too late. Twenty-two years late for Sandra to

express any sort of sympathy or apology. Where did she hide her sorrow or compassion the night it mattered? He blinked away an image—sitting next to his brother Joe in the Marshall police station. The adults, police in and out of uniform, had told them to wait. Stunned and tired, they followed directions and stayed close to each other. Two men led their mother across the other side of the narrow room. For one long moment she turned her face to them. Her face was blank, no sorrow at what she'd done and no concern for her sons. He and Joe could have been blocks of wood for all the interest evident in her features. In one disinterested look she changed from "Mom" to "Sandra."

He drew a deep breath, held it long enough to override the instinct to lash back with reminders of the worst night of their lives. His outbursts of frustration and anger through the years, during prison visits or when she insisted on hugging him like he remained a small boy, didn't solve anything. Nothing could bring Sam back. Nothing would change the past enough for him to say, "I love you, Dad," when it mattered the most.

"I've got to go. I'm scheduled to assist on an early surgery." He dumped his breakfast in the trash. The two bites he'd managed to swallow supplied objects to Apprehension to juggle instead of nutrition. Eating would wait until Sandra wasn't asking him for the impossible.

"Call me if you hear more about Lawrence. Please, David."

He aimed a sigh away from the phone. Agreeing would placate Sandra. He didn't plan to seek information on Larry. No harm in forwarding stray facts if they fell into his possession. "I can let you know. Call his family."

He wanted information about and from Maylee, not her attacker. He needed to hear words from her lips, see with his eyes. No, he'd not see her, not until after surgery and clinic hours. Detective Wilson mentioned reports and interviews in a casual manner. The department would keep her busy well into today. He'd need to trust her partner about her health and safety. And hold his question of why she'd been a target.

"He's a decent man, David. Don't paint him as a monster."

He pressed his lips tight to smother "sick" and "stupid," the two descriptors currently wrestling on the back of his tongue. At this point, his honest assessment would only lead to another in a long history of circular arguments. After swallowing them away, he mumbled a line about the hospital and ended the call.

The best thing for him today would be work. He'd immerse himself in patient concerns and avoid news reports. He'd be polite, wait a decent interval. If he left a voicemail between surgeries and office hours she'd have time to fill out at least a portion of the required incident paperwork. He tucked the business card left by Detective Wilson into his wallet and headed for the hospital.

****

Maylee dumped warm, flat soda down the sink and muttered a curse. The wall clock proclaimed the time as 1400 hours. Her body disagreed, responding with shorter and shorter intervals of alertness with each dose of caffeine. If, or rather when, she settled in a bed, she expected a full day would pass in oblivion.

Her soft rant, laced with adjectives usually associated with military men or frustrated sports figures, stayed below a normal whisper, not intended for others to hear. On a rational level she understood why her superiors confined her to desk duty until further notice. Another slice of her personality, the impulsive, impatient portion, itched to interview Thompson with all the techniques used only in the movies. If he resisted, or raised so much as a finger in threat, she'd opt for CIA rumored methods.

"The very reason we have rules." She pulled a bleach scented wipe from the container. She rubbed away coffee and faint food stains from the snack room table.

Justice. Barbara. She shook her head and scrubbed harder. Did it really start all those years ago, when her father refused to prosecute Dr. Saterro for vehicular homicide? The case notes available contained conflicting eye-witness accounts. The accident reconstruction didn't draw a definite conclusion. Prosecution would have wasted time and taxpayer money in addition to ruining Dr. Saterro's life.

What sort of man held a grudge for more than a dozen years? Did a person in touch with reality pass an appetite for revenge on to the next generation? She sighed. Thompson would be one for the psychiatrists to puzzle over.

"You must be bored." Tom entered the small area and opened the fridge.

"I'm coping. Watching Thompson sleep on the video feed isn't the most exciting of tasks."

"Make you jealous?"

She attacked a smear of encrusted food on a plastic

chair. "Have you ever noticed the similarity of three day old pizza sauce and dry blood?"

"You're avoiding the question."

"Am I tired? Yes." She skimmed the wipe over the chair back. "And you? You've been at this since…well, almost as long as I have."

"To copy a phrase, I'm coping." He twisted the cap off a bottle of cola and took a big swallow. "I see you've removed Tony's picture from your wall display."

"We've made a solid arrest. Tony never had a motive." She wadded the wipe and tossed it into the trash. "Don't get me wrong. I'm glad he's not in my family. And I'm convinced he's slippery and frequently steps outside of the law. Has he had a tax audit?"

"I like the way you think." Tom cut his laugh off short. "The team called as they left Thompson's house. They're bringing back a full van."

Weariness vanished quicker than a germ under her sanitizing wipe. "How much do the rules allow you to tell me?"

"Prescription drugs. Computer. File of newspaper clippings." He took another drink, tapped his chest in a dramatic pause, and burped. "Knife collection."

She focused on the first item. "Did we draw enough blood? He behaved drunk instead of high."

"Blood alcohol report's back. Four times legal limit."

"Geeze. I'm related to people who pass out well before then."

Tom laughed. "It's time for you to go home. Re-discover sleep. Jamison will drive you."

"How long for the lab to get quantities on those

prescription drugs?"

"Patience, Morgan. Now get your personal stuff together and go home."

She started to open her mouth, managed to shut it before a stupid word escaped. Her rental car remained at the apartment. She'd come to headquarters early this morning in the passenger seat of a cruiser, her knees sandwiched between the computer and bean bag gun. "Right. And you?"

"Following orders." He dropped the empty soda bottle into the recycle bin. "Don't be afraid of missing any of the good parts. Thompson's lawyer stopped in, managed to keep him awake for five minutes, and scheduled a return for early morning."

"Exact time?" Maylee's long time experience with lawyers made her understand "early" to an attorney and a detective to be far from equal.

"Seven-thirty. Go home. Sleep."

Her phone chimed with an incoming text and she sneaked a peek at the number. *Dave. Third one since eleven.*

"Good work, Morgan." Tom tossed two mints on the table in front of her. "Talk to your neighbor. Thank him for calling it in. We did."

"How much? What did he see?" They'd not let her read any of the statements from her neighbors. Another portion of the rules and procedure designed to protect her and the integrity of the testimony. At least Mrs. Gossen wasn't in the building. Her statement would be as long as *Doctor Zhivago*.

"Enough to call."

A minute later, with Tom out of sight and hopefully out of hearing, she tapped the code to return

Dave's call.

"This is Dr. Holmes."

"No voice mail?"

"You got lucky. How are you? Injured? Buried under paperwork?"

She leaned against the counter and turned a laugh into a silent smile. "Close to the last option. As to my health—nothing a long nap won't cure."

"You're…good, better than good, excellent."

What had he started to say? Did he abort a standard statement claiming she was lucky not to be coming out of surgery for a gunshot wound? Or something more personal? "I understand I owe you thanks. For calling it in."

"The car panic button was a nice touch."

"A person works with the tools at hand." She stifled a yawn.

"I'd like to talk. Over supper would be good."

"I can't comment on active investigations." She repeated the cardinal rule without actually thinking. Friends, family, even the ones who should have respect for confidentiality engrained to the core seemed to require a reminder.

"I'm thinking we can find other things to discuss. You're a clever interrogator. Tomorrow?"

"Hmmm. I should be available." After several hours of sleep and another shift of paperwork she should be ready for a good meal.

"Good. My place. Seven thirty?"

His place? She swallowed down the wrong response. "I'd be honored. Do you actually cook or merely conjure up mouthwatering aromas like a chemistry lab?"

"Obviously, we hang out in different chem labs. I've got to go. Seven thirty."

"Got it."

Chapter Eighteen

Maylee lifted Angel, her Glock 19, out of the hip holster and slipped it into the lockable drawer. For the previous twenty minutes, since walking into her apartment, she'd debated about wearing her weapon to supper.

House rule. No handguns. She turned the lock and poked the key into a pocket of her safari shorts. A good guest respected the host. The advice sounded similar to hints for contemporary manners sprinkled in magazine columns. Out of habit, she tugged the hem of last year's Poppy Run T-shirt down to cover the belt she didn't wear.

A few moments later she smiled in front of his door. He opened after the first knock. "Hi, Chef Holmes."

Dave stepped back, opened the door wider, and gestured her inside. He inspected her in silence until she glanced down to check if her socks matched.

"Are you armed?" He sent the words out as tentative as a dog's first sniff of a stranger's hand.

"Allow me to repeat from another encounter." She reached out with her right arm. "Right arm. Great tool for all sorts of things. Left arm is a mirror image. Angel's taking a nap in her usual sleeping quarters."

"Good." He stepped forward and placed his hands around her upper arms. "Do you mind? I'm grateful you didn't get hurt."

"Control. Training." She omitted the dry mouth, trembling, and cold sweat attack after she turned a cuffed Thompson over to the patrol officers and an EMT. "It's over. History." *Until next time.* She refused to think about the possible personal hazards she'd face on the job in the future. After a few months on patrol she'd learned certain alleys of thinking led only to poor sleep.

Without direction from her brain, her hands rested on his shoulders, creating enough heat for them to glow.

"May I?" He skimmed his hands up, exploring with a gentle, skimming touch until he cupped her cheeks.

She stared into his eyes, forgot to count the seconds like a good contest demands, and fumbled a heartbeat when he leaned in for the kiss. His lips caressed, requested, and rested for a moment. Maylee opened to him, responded with a greedy mouth. Her mind twirled off into a fantasy world where kisses tasted like spun sugar and fingers rubbed skin as soft as spring sunshine.

Moments, or perhaps hours later, he eased away, rested his forehead against hers, and whispered into the tiny space between them. "Thank you."

She panted air back into her chest. "You're welcome."

He laughed, darted his lips in for a short punctuation mark against hers. An instant later he pushed the door closed. "Show's over."

She licked orphaned lips and recovered enough senses to identify the sights and smells of beef roast and fresh biscuits. She breathed a little deeper and searched for a name to the spice scenting the air. Rosemary? Could a culinary herb make people daring? "No encore?"

He lifted one side of a closed smile. "Come. Sit. I took the liberty of asking Detective Wilson about your drinking habits." He held out one of the mismatched vinyl chairs and pointed to a bottle of an award winning red from a prominent Missouri winery. "I'll be your server tonight. Do you want a detailed menu?"

"No." She sat in front of a place set with red and white stoneware. "I'll have the house special. And a side of conversation."

He busied his hands with the corkscrew. "Exactly the menu for this evening. Let me fill our glasses and plates before you put on the interrogation hat."

"No hurry." She fastened her gaze on his hands, moved it to his mouth, and skimmed it over pale blue polo shirt and jeans snug across his butt. *Complete package.* The memory of the kiss sent a tremble to her fingers.

Half an hour later Maylee laid flatware across a plate wearing a few drops of au jus and two specks of carrot. "Delicious. Every bite."

"We have dessert." Dave stood and gathered up their plates.

"I don't need more calories." She sipped from her wine glass. During the meal they'd compared college tales, political opinions, and hopes for the Cardinals to bring home another World Series trophy. "Where did you learn to cook? I didn't find a culinary school in your background."

"Figured you ran one." He removed two small dishes from the freezer and busied his hands topping them. "Was it a boring report?"

"For the most part." The only questionable puzzle piece—why Robert Kale as emergency contact—was answered when we ran Sandra's background check later.

"Here you go, designed to melt into the crevices between the rest of the meal." He set a dish of vanilla ice cream dusted with cinnamon in front of her. He waited for her to take a bite before he spoke again. "Aunt Joan taught cooking to all of us. She insisted we be able to maintain our own apartment. I also think she wanted a little help around the house. Cooking wasn't the only skill she made us practice. Once, after an indoor skirmish with food coloring in our squirt guns, cleaning turned into a team sport. All our future battles were outside."

Maylee choked, swallowed, and exhaled. "Don't tell my brothers. Or nephews. They'd try it."

"They missed it?"

"It must have been one of the few things not in their repertoire. I learned early to be sparse on details to parents if I tagged along on their adventures." She allowed a brief, fond memory of Matt defending her when one of his friends accused her of throwing a football like a girl.

"Sandra called today." He rested his spoon beside the ice cream. "She calls every day. Too much actually. But this time her comments raised questions."

She nodded and remained quiet. While she welcomed the several times a week calls from her mother, she understood Dave and Sandra maintained a completely different relationship.

"She raced through a list of charges against Larry. I

didn't expect it to be so long. Or to include murder. Can you explain? Or is it against your department rules?"

"The charges are public record." She set the spoon inside the empty bowl and leaned back in her chair. Dave didn't have the background information to tie the attack in the parking lot to his boss's death. She studied his face, noting the compressed mouth and steady, questioning eyes. "The charges against Lawrence Thompson include crimes on two different nights. Highlights for the first, surrounding Dr. Saterro's death, begin with pre-meditated murder. They continue to include illegal transport of a body and end at the cemetery with the desecration of a grave. Actually, I think the word 'littering' would be more accurate. He didn't vandalize any stones when he disposed of the body."

Dave laced his hands on the table and squeezed until his knuckles faded. "Larry killed Dr. Saterro? Has he confessed? What about..." He gestured toward the window. "Out there?"

"Threatening a police officer. Brandishing weapons."

"Plural?"

"That's all I can confirm. Thompson's pleading and bargaining with the prosecutor's office continues. He claims no memory of the murder, transport, or staging in the cemetery." She pressed her hands tight and flat on her thighs as bits and pieces of the events replayed. If she made the mistake of closing her eyes, she'd see the flash of the combat knife blade as it moved in and out of the security light beam. Or maybe this time her mind would dwell on the dark shape of the revolver in Thompson's right hand.

"Will he get a deal?" Dave leaned forward while relaxing his clasped fingers. "Sandra expressed concern about his medication before this all happened. Nothing I could do. Nothing anyone could. Will he get medical help?"

"He's in a safe place. Yes, he'll get medical help. And dry out." She measured her next words. The evidence technicians and crime lab personnel continued their procedures connecting items from Larry's house and truck to the Saterro homicide. A thick file of letters, copies of those sent to the prosecutor's office, Dr. Saterro, Barbara's parents, and insurance companies through the years, were catching a lot of attention. However, they were outnumbered by correspondence never mailed to the same addresses plus a judge, a suburban police chief, and newspapers.

Maylee rubbed her arms as a chill skimmed her skin. A deliberate breath and blink did nothing this time to quell the regret they'd not been able to obtain a warrant sooner. "I'm not privy to the details. The more charges he confesses to the better the deal. Personally, I'm hoping he pleads out to avoid a trial."

He steepled his index fingers and nodded. "Make a deal. Exactly what Sandra did. I think it turned out to be her only kind decision in the whole rotten mess. Plead to a lesser charge to keep me off the stand."

An invisible fist slammed into Maylee's chest. "You…you witnessed?"

"Statement is sealed. A minor and all. Sandra planned it. The gun rested on her lap long before Sam walked in the door. It didn't make any difference in the end." He paused, swallowed, and stared into her face.

He's calm. Rehearsed?

"I got permission and read the reports last month. A single shot severed the external carotid artery. Dad was beyond hope before he crumpled to the floor. I panicked. Or gave into survival instinct. Either way you spin it, I ran away. I sprinted to our room and managed to keep Joe out of sight and quiet." He blinked in a flurry before turning away. "Not a proper good-by. I've always felt he saw me as he died. Then again…it might be a child's fantasy."

She reached out and covered his hands with her own.

"When you pulled your gun on Larry—it turned into split screen television. Reality on one side and…the night in Marshall—in terrible living color—crowding in on the other."

"I'm not Sandra." She rubbed her thumb against his smooth, strong skin.

He glanced at the ceiling, appeared to gather his emotions into a tight male bundle, and turned back to her. "And I'm not a child. It's time to rewrite my unspoken rules. Will you help me break a few preconceived ideas?"

"I'd be honored What do you have in mind?"

"This." He stood, drawing her up also, and stepped to within inches of her body.

An instant later his lips melted into hers and carried her thoughts to the top of an amusement park ride. She responded to each millimeter of skin, wrestled his tongue with her own, and begged for more. When they broke the kiss she found her fingers threaded in his hair, reveling in the fine texture. In her core, the tiny spark of fascination, or lust, or something deeper, swelled into a steady candle flame. "Your expertise goes beyond the kitchen."

"Would you care for a further demonstration?"

Desire wrestled with caution as she stared at him in best contest form and counted the seconds in silence. Her body betrayed her inner turmoil with a tremor as his finger traced a spiral on her neck, awakening distracting passions. It wasn't fair. But then, did she want him to follow the usual rules?

When he blinked, she closed the tiny gap between them and brushed her lips across his jaw. She savored him for a long moment before sighing out a single word. "Later."

****

Dave twirled his wine glass once more before setting it on the table. His methods of keeping his hands occupied while remaining several feet away from Maylee were nearly exhausted. "Have we anesthetized it yet?"

"The elephant? Tiger? Yeti?" She grasped a decorative pillow and pushed it between her back and the low arm of the out-of-date couch.

"The beast prowling between us. I wasn't aware you believed in yeti?"

"I like a touch of exotic in my life." She smiled before pushing one hand through her hair. "You have satisfied my curiosity regarding your relationship with weapons. For tonight."

He swallowed down a lump of lust climbing his throat. She looked so inviting, curled up at the end of one of the most uncomfortable pieces of furniture in existence. He crossed the space between them and settled beside her feet. "I went on the computer today."

"So? Wouldn't it be more newsworthy if you

didn't?"

"Another point for you." He licked an index finger and added to the haphazard, invisible tally started while they loaded the dishwasher. "Actually, I visited a new-to-me website. I signed up for the Poppy Run."

"There's not much time left to train."

"Two full weeks. I'll need a running buddy. Any idea who I should ask?" He reached over, tucked a strand of hair behind her ear, and admired the small pearl decorating her lobe.

"I might know someone." She reached up and wrapped her hand around his wrist. "Are you averse to training with a girl?"

"Depends. Is she wearing short hair that shines like pecans in sunlight? Does she smile easy? Run on the most perfect legs in St. Louis?"

She smiled for an instant before it changed into a whisper of a laugh. "Flatterer."

"Tomorrow morning. Unless the hospital calls?"

"How convenient. I don't have to report back to paperwork mountain until Monday morning." She guided his hand toward her lips until he could feel her breath heat his skin

Temptation had a new name, and he grew weaker against it by the heartbeat.

"And if the hospital does call?"

"Then we reschedule to afternoon." He reached beside him on the cushion until his hand closed around a sock-encased foot. "I warned you my schedule is erratic."

"Complements mine, I suspect."

A few minutes later her bare feet rested on his lap. Dave worked his thumbs in circles against smooth skin from her ankle to toes.

She closed her eyes and sighed. "I could get used to this. Did they teach massage tricks in med school?"

"It fascinated me one summer. Read up on it. Practiced on skeptical relatives."

"Since you mentioned family." She opened her eyes. "How well do you like baseball?"

"I don't play it well."

"All you need to do is watch the Cardinals. At the stadium. Surrounded by assorted Morgans."

He switched his hands to her other ankle. He recited several of the bones under his thumbs: tarsus, calcaneus, and talus, to subdue the urge to drop her foot and kiss her senseless. "Ms. Morgan, are you asking me on a date?"

"I've an ulterior motive. One of the family wagers I mentioned."

"Now you've got my full attention." He abandoned the massage and moved his hands to either side of her rib cage. "We need to get better acquainted before I inject myself into your family. Training runs. Meals. Conversations into the night. Maybe a movie."

"Sounds intense."

"Exclusive." He pulled her forward until her buttocks nestled on his lap. "Both ways. I'm not a double standard sort of person."

"Two weeks." She touched her forehead to his.

He moved his face, kissed her lightly, and whispered. "Renewable."

Chapter Nineteen

Claiming the window seat, Maylee turned a few degrees to better pattern her gaze over the other riders in the light rail car. Her fellow passengers, many dressed for and already commenting on the afternoon Cardinals' game, were more interesting than the rail yards and scattered industrial buildings outside. Especially fascinating was her seat partner, Dave. "Nervous?"

"About meeting your family? No." He brushed one hand across his new red shirt.

"Something's got your upper lip sweating. Is it your allergy?" She felt the reassuring presence of Angel, her handgun, holstered at her hip as the train swayed. A few days ago, in deference to Dave's attempt to come to acceptance with her weapon, they'd decided to refer to the situation in medical terms.

He started to raise his hand to his mouth and stopped. "The department must save money on lie detectors with you around."

"Talk to me, Doc."

"I want an extension. On our agreement."

She glanced down, reluctant to allow him to see the joy sweeping across her eyes. It would be easy to give him an immediate answer. But her partner's frequent reminder to exercise patience and her natural inclination to assert independence prevailed.

"Because?"

"Interior conflict." He paused and gathered a deep breath. "When you're in sight, my body parts toss emotions like salad ingredients. I'm asking for more time to get them settled and named. Prime candidates at the moment are fleeting lust and forever love."

She held her lips tight and straight. With increasing frequency, she juggled similar emotions. Currently, their relationship resembled many of their runs—exhilarating while in progress and deflating when they parted. "Same terms? How long?"

"Exclusive. Same terms." He picked up her left hand from her lap and sandwiched it lightly. "Six months? Until the end of the year? Open ended?"

"Interesting idea. I'll need to think about this." She closed her eyes for a long blink. Her attraction for Dave jumped from interesting to spectacular at times like this. "End of the second inning—I'll give you a chance to retract your offer after you meet my family."

"Could I get you to reconsider?" He leaned close and whispered. "Bottom of the first?"

A shiver of excitement danced across her shoulder at the nearness of his lips. She swallowed down the impulse to accept his terms this instant. As he backed away, she exhaled a sigh in chorus with the train gliding into their stop.

A few minutes later, Maylee held Dave's hand and led them across the street to the sunny plaza outside the downtown stadium. Near-life-size statues of Hall of Fame members provided meeting places for groups of all sizes. She guided them directly to the Bob Gibson statue and an excited cluster of dark haired fans.

Maylee handled the introductions and allowed her

grin free rein as Dave shook hands, repeated names, and appeared to ignore the general chatter between Morgan siblings and their partners.

"Welcome to the circus." Dianne extended one hand.

Dave lifted the matriarch's hand and brushed a kiss across the top. "I'll stay alert, Madam Ringmaster."

"You overestimate me, young man." She laughed and tugged on Maylee's sleeve. "It's about time you won the annual wager."

"The straggler arrives." Steve, the oldest Morgan brother, pointed toward an approaching couple dressed in the unofficial fan uniform of khaki bottoms and red shirts.

No. He didn't. Maylee stared, her brother Matt escorted Kate Allegro toward them.

"Problem?" Dave stage whispered.

"It doesn't concern you." She found a smile and greeted the new arrivals. Later, after she confirmed an extension of her agreement with Dave, she'd caution her brother not to break Kate's heart when the army ordered him to a remote base.

"Sis." Matt bumped her fist in greeting. "Who's the blond?"

Epilogue

November

Dave jogged beside Maylee in the cool, dark, evening air. Small, bright beams from their new headband flashlights swayed ahead of them. Like their bodies, the light rays remained close but not touching. He matched her stride and tried not to be obvious as he glanced toward the street on the south border of Saxon Park.

Not yet. He prepared to run another lap, their fifth.

"You're distracted." Her voice emerged clear and steady, without a hint of physical exertion two-thirds of a mile later.

"Busy day." He used a simple half truth. Two surgeries this morning and clinic patients this afternoon added up to a full, but not hectic, day at work. The cause of his disorganized thoughts, Maylee, moved beside him. All the careful conversations he'd rehearsed in today's quiet moments vanished as they trotted side by side.

"Next race is coming up Saturday morning. You're off your pace tonight."

"I confess. I've got something on my mind." He panted for the next half dozen strides after talking.

"Discuss it over supper?"

"No." He gestured to the plaza area where benches,

oversized flowerpots, and small statues waited under scattered lights. He'd begin now, before his courage failed, regardless of when the others arrived. "Bench. This lap."

"You'll never catch me at this rate." She sprinted ahead and didn't slow until circling back to one of the far backless seats.

She was right. He shook his head and tried not to care that in each of the three charity runs they'd participated in she'd beat him by five minutes or more. His times improved, either from the consistent practice or the track coach advice she dropped like candy bits before or after runs. But he hadn't caught her, yet.

"What's on your mind, Doc?" She propped one foot on the concrete seat and leaned forward in a graceful stretch.

You. He stopped his tongue before raw words escaped. She deserved the best. He needed to calm for a moment and get this right. He tapered his jogging in place, halted and gained another pair of vital seconds clicking off their headband flashlights. "Living arrangements. I want to discuss them."

She raised her brows in a silent question and flashed him one of her faster smirks. "My lease expires in three months. I want my next place to allow pets."

Did she suspect? How much? "Could you...would you?" He skimmed his cold, sweaty palms down the front of his running suit. "Could you keep Angel out of the bedroom? And marry me?"

Her mouth formed a perfect circle for an instant before her laugh danced into the quiet air.

A flash of heat engulfed his neck, and he exhaled silent thanks for soft lighting. "I said that all wrong. Do over?"

"And spoil a fine story for the grandkids?"

"Huh? What?" Reality slammed into his brain and he reached out to her. Whether he lifted or she jumped didn't matter. She was in his arms, her hands laced behind his neck. He caressed her lips with his. She tasted wonderful; all mint mouthwash, fresh air, and home. Greed pounced as he deepened the kiss and she welcomed him. He wanted more of her. He wanted her forever. Or until they needed to breathe again. He scattered another trio of kisses on her neck before speaking. "Detective, may I take that as an affirmative?"

She cradled his chin in one hand and stared into his eyes. "I've been waiting for you."

"I intend to make it worthwhile." He stroked her back, lingered his palms at her shoulder blades. She felt so warm and vibrant. He hesitated to break contact for even an instant. A sound from the street caused him to look over as a long, black shape pulled to the curb. "Pardon me." He leaned in to give her a quick peck on the cheek before he dropped to one knee and started digging into the key pouch of his running shoe. "I can make this official."

A few moments later, they walked hand in hand toward the gleaming limo discharging the Morgan family. Dave talked close to her ear. "The party's at Uncle Bob's."

"One thing." She stopped and tugged him to a halt out of her mother's hearing range. "I'm keeping my name. Witnesses would collapse laughing at Detective Holmes."

He stared at her, counting the seconds. He blinked

first, at twelve. "I expected as much. I, however, will name the dog Sherlock."

A word about the author…

Raised in a household full of books, it was only natural that Ellen Parker grew up with a book in her hand. She turned to writing as a second career and enjoys spinning the type of story which appeals to more than one generation. She encourages readers to share her work with mother or daughter—or both.

When not guiding characters to their "happily ever after" she's likely reading, tending her postage-stamp garden, or walking in the neighborhood. She currently lives in St. Louis. You can find her on the web at: www.ellenparkerwrites.wordpress.com or on Facebook at: www.facebook.com/ellenparkerwrites.

Thank you for purchasing
this publication of The Wild Rose Press, Inc.

If you enjoyed the story, we would appreciate your
letting others know by leaving a review.

For other wonderful stories,
please visit our on-line bookstore at
www.thewildrosepress.com.

For questions or more information
contact us at
info@thewildrosepress.com.

The Wild Rose Press, Inc.
www.thewildrosepress.com

Stay current with The Wild Rose Press, Inc.

Like us on Facebook

https://www.facebook.com/TheWildRosePress

And Follow us on Twitter
https://twitter.com/WildRosePress